A Cry in the Mist

OTHER TITLES BY DOUG WOODWARD

You Took the Kids Where? Adventuring While Your Children Are Young

Wherever Waters Flow: A Lifelong Love Affair with Wild Rivers

A Cry in the Mist

& Other Needmore Valley Tales

Doug Woodward

HEADWATERS PUBLISHING

HeadwatersPublishing.com

A Cry in the Mist and Other Needmore Valley Tales
Copyright ©2020 by Doug Woodward

Cover & text design by Lynn "Cricket" Woodward. WoodwardCreative.com

All photos by Doug Woodward except author photo by Cricket Woodward and illustrator photo provided.

Introduction photos: Looking upriver from the Needmore swinging bridge. Lower Brush Creek Road in Needmore. High Lonesome road sign.

Headwaters Publishing
412 Thunder Creek
Franklin, NC 28734
whitewater6@gmail.com
HeadwatersPublishing.com

First Edition: 2020

Library of Congress Cataloging-in-Publication Data — Fiction

Woodward, Doug, 1936 –

A Cry in the Mist and Other Needmore Valley Tales/
by Doug Woodward.—1st ed.

106 p; 12 photos; 21.5 cm

ISBN 978-0-9779314-1-5 (trade paperback)

1. Appalachian Mountains—History 1710-1997—Fiction. 2. Cherokee people—Fiction.
3. Women activists—Fiction. 4. Irish immigrants—Fiction. 5. North Carolina—Fiction.

D.D. Classification — Fiction

This book is dedicated to all those families — past and present —
who have loved living in Needmore,
despite the hard work and frustration that could be a part of that life.

And particularly to Joyce Breedlove Starr, who once lived in Needmore,
and who encouraged me to continue writing these stories
after listening to me read at the old Rickman's Store.
Keep on clogging, Joyce!

∞

Contents

A Word About Needmore

DOWN BY THE RIVER IS A ROAD SIGN — the words read simply, "Needmore" and "High Lonesome" — at the spot where that gravel road claws its way up the mountain from the river valley. Except for the names of the roads, it could be a signpost in any North Carolina town. However, this one is different. The settlement has vanished, but its main street remains.

Needmore, the remote remnant of a once-thriving community, borders the Little Tennessee River in northern Macon and southern Swain Counties, starting near High Lonesome Road where Tellico Creek empties its waters into the Little T, and running with the free-flowing river until it dies in the backwaters of Fontana Lake. Along the way are such names as Licklog Creek, Painter (Panther) Branch, Rattlesnake Creek, Bull Hollow, Sawmill Creek and, of course, High Lonesome, boasting the most stolen road sign in western North Carolina. The names alone take you back into another era.

Needmore is wild country, wilder than it was a century ago, and quite possibly the most untouched stretch of major river in the southern Appalachians. It is unique and irreplaceable. Three and one-half miles of the road are unpaved. The pristine water in this part of the river supports endangered aquatic species and rare plants grow on its banks. The branches of trees from each side of the road beckon to each other, forming a shady canopy appreciated by all who will gather there.

There is a reason for the obvious lack of development along the river in the Needmore corridor. Sixty years ago, following completion of the major dams in the surrounding watershed, Nantahala Power and Light Co. thought they might need one more dam and began acquiring both land and purchase options on property that fell on or below the 1,980-foot contour elevation. Each time NP&L did a cost analysis, they found construction of the dam to be uneconomical as did Duke Power (now Duke Energy) when they acquired NP&L.

Finally, in the early 1990s, when Duke turned the Needmore property over to their development arm, Crescent Resources, to begin sales, the picture began to heat up. Former landowners, or their descendants, who had previously been told that they had no choice but to sell or sign an option because their land was going to be underwater, wanted their property back. And others who enjoyed the beauty and remote feel of this wild country did not want to see it chopped up for development.

Smelling a possible legal mess, Duke indicated that the property could be purchased and kept intact. The Land Trust for the Little Tennessee (now Mainspring) stepped in and led a coalition of hunters, fishermen, campers, boaters and others in raising funds to save the Needmore Tract. The price was met, LTLT took temporary control and eventually the huge piece of land — more than 4,400 acres — bordering the river was turned over to the NC Wildlife Resources Commission.

Needmore is dear to the hearts of many of us who live in or near this corridor and certainly my own heart is one of these. Whether I'm biking the twelve-mile loop which the swinging bridge connects, hiking to the ruins of the old Hampton farmstead, or just sitting with my feet in the river, writing one of these stories, I can't imagine Needmore being turned into a paved thoroughfare with the widening and straightening that all such NC Department of Transportation projects require.

I will not pretend that mine is the only viewpoint — it is not. There are those who still live on the side roads of Needmore who would never have been submerged under the proposed lake, but would have had isolated lake front property had the dam been built. Some of them commute to Franklin for work and would love to see the gravel road become paved.

Yet I would caution all of us to consider the aesthetic cost of such a change — the great increase in traffic, the loss of solitude for fishermen, hunters and descendants of Needmore families who still visit the remains of their old homesteads, and the loss of perhaps the most uniquely beautiful stretch of river in these eastern Appalachian mountains.

∞

Each of these tales has a Needmore connection, some set in the heart of the corridor and others nearby. Each tale also has a young woman as the main character — one that is quite capable of taking charge of her life and of being a leader of others. I have a particular passion for seeing women triumph over prejudice after so many centuries of paternalism. Also, I have a deep interest in writing stories that do not glorify war or violence and have tried to think and write with that intent in these tales.

And did the events in these stories really happen? You'll need to judge that for yourself. Though they are written as products of my imagination, the tales are woven around geographical facts and occasional real persons who emerge from history. There is always the possibility of more truth being present than you might at first guess.

∞

As a writer of non-fiction all my life, creating tales is new territory for me. I would like to thank all descendants of the Needmore families for allowing me to tread on their sacred ground.

And the real history of Needmore will always be more interesting than fiction. I highly recommend that the reader investigate the following sources:

ReflectionsofOldeSwain.blogspot.com
Wendy Meyers has delved into the history of the people and places that once made Needmore a bustling community by interviewing family descendants, researching old newspaper accounts and collecting photographs taken during the heyday of Needmore. Her blog reaches well beyond Needmore, to the towns drowned beneath Fontana Lake and to every corner of Swain County.

AlarkaExpeditions.com
Brent and Angela Faye Martin have a vast knowledge of the diversity of flora and fauna that live in this riparian corridor, as well as the forgotten trails and roads that connect the history of the region. They will take you by water or by foot on a personally guided look at Needmore.

WildSouth.org
Lamar Marshall is a historian whose knowledge reaches back to the time of the Cherokee and beyond. He has researched and mapped many of the ancient sites in the Needmore corridor.

Against All Odds
1710

"UNFAIR! UNFAIR!" MUTTERED TUTI from her vantage point on the cliff that towered above the river. She was watching the young men from the surrounding villages vying with each other to gain the lead in the annual skill and endurance race. Yes, these youths were in prime condition, having trained for at least the past year for the big event. But — and this observation had rankled her sense of fairness — out of nearly seventy eager competitors, there was not a female among them.

Tuti — meaning "snowbird" in Cherokee — was as beautiful as her name. Her long braids shone a glistening black and hung nearly to her hips. High cheekbones gave her a regal look and complemented a compassionate mouth. Her skin showed not a blemish and her teeth sparkled when she smiled, which was often. Whenever she came close in conversation, you could catch the fragrance of the birch twig upon which she chewed. But she had an impulsive side to her, as she sometimes spoke before grasping the effect of her own words.

The grueling race — tougher than any ultra marathon we know today — would finish in Tuti's village of Allijay after the runners had overcome many daunting obstacles along the way. Tuti had chosen a vantage point where she could see the young men make their third crossing of the great river, the one that whites would later name Little Tennessee. It was near dusk when the last runner swam the terrific current and scrambled out of the water. Tuti sighed and followed the familiar trail toward home.

Exasperated looks from her grandmother, mother, and sisters greeted her in the common cooking area of the village. "Tuti, you've done it again! You know what a huge feast we must put on for our guests tonight and all the work involved. Then you disappear — just to watch those handsome young studs run by."

"No mother, it wasn't that," Tuti replied, although she had to admit to herself that the runners had prompted some delightful stirrings in her belly now that she had passed her fourteenth winter. "And I did work hard well before most others were up, building fires and stripping venison. But it's … it's just not right for this to be an all-boys event — the most important contest of the year — when I'm sure that there are girls that could do it too."

"What you mean is, 'Tuti,' not 'girls.'"

"Yes Mother, I know I could finish — if I had time to practice — and probably finish ahead of some of the young braves."

"My, what grandiose dreams you have, my dear. Talk with Grandfather later, but right now get this batch of corn into the coals and come right back."

The size of the crowd was tremendous and they were in high spirits as they ate and prepared to toast the winners of the day-long obstacle race. The women in Tuti's family made sure that Tuti was kept busy with serving duties as long as there was anyone still eating. She barely heard the names of the winners and the congratulatory words as each was recognized, but her heart yearned to be in the circle of those who had finished the race.

Early morning saw the departure of most of the competitors and their families as they headed for their home villages. With a morning break in her chores, Tuti sought the company of her mother's father.

"Grandfather, has a girl ever competed in the Grand River Run?" Tuti bluntly asked.

Her grandfather pondered the question for a time before answering. "Not in my memory, granddaughter," he replied.

"Well, I want to be in it next year. Will they let me?" she blurted out.

"Tuti, I know the desire burns within you, but there are many skills you need in that race besides running, my granddaughter. It is not for me to say. Why don't you speak with Sadayi? As head of our clan, she will know how to answer you."

There were many clean-up duties from the night before and Tuti was busy well into the afternoon — but she had sent word to Sadayi, respectfully asking for an audience. Evening came, and she timidly approached Sadayi's hut with a gift of roasted mountain quail.

Having satisfied the formalities, Tuti expressed her desires and asked her questions. Then Sadayi spoke. "Answer me with a truthful tongue. Why would you want to do such a thing? Is it to be near to the young braves?"

"Oh no! It's the race. I know I can do it, and that I would make our village proud."

"Tuti, let me tell you this. You know that the Cherokee hold women in high regard and that the leader of each clan is a woman. However, with a few exceptions, our tasks are divided among men and women and rarely do we deviate from that tradition. It may be that your wish could be granted, however unlikely, but surely you will have to show more than desire, and this will be a matter for the Council to decide."

Tuti knew that Sadayi spoke the truth, but she still tucked away a glimmer of hope. The Council would not meet until the moon was full, and would they even consider such a trivial matter as this?

Two weeks passed before the moon was round and brilliant, and the Council was busy with plans for the new townhouse. They would discuss such details as which trees were to be cut for building, when would the earth and rock haulers have the mound to proper height, who would be responsible for each aspect of the work and more. Tuti had little hope that her request would be discussed.

The Council met for two full days and evenings. Runners were seen going to and from the site of the new townhouse as well as the nearby forest. Food was prepared and brought in. At last the meetings came to an end and the Council members retired to their own dwellings.

The village was abuzz with talk of how the new townhouse would appear when finished.

So no one was more surprised than Tuti when she was summoned to appear at Sadayi's lodge that evening.

"Yes, my dear, the Council did take time to discuss your request." Tuti shivered with apprehension.

Sadayi went on. "I told them of the great desire that you have to do this thing, but several said it would be impossible for a girl to reach the same level of skill as our young braves. However, there were some who supported the idea and, in the end, a consensus was reached. It was decided that you — or any other young woman who wishes to compete in the Grand River Run — must first pass a qualifying test. This test would be conducted five moons from now, and consist of three of the more difficult tasks that will occur in the actual race. Does that sound fair?"

Tuti almost blurted out, "No, that doesn't sound fair — none of the braves have to pass such a test to enter the race!" but held her impulsive tongue just in time. She realized that she had just been given an opportunity that easily could have been denied and that it was up to her to prove herself worthy of this honor.

"Thank you, Sadayi. With a grateful heart, thank you."

∞

"Oh my," thought Tuti, "Now the challenge is mine alone. I have always been tough and I don't give up easily, but I must find out what I can and can't do, and determine a way to overcome the 'can't do's'. I *know* it's possible."

Word of Tuti's challenge spread quickly through Allijay, with a mix of skepticism and curiosity. Every spare moment that Tuti had — and there were not many in her busy family and village life —

was spent in improving her strength and stamina. In her chore routines, she always chose the most demanding work and could often be seen carrying rocks to the site of the new mound. Each day that she had the time, she would run, gasping for breath, to the top of Kalasunyi, the towering cliffs behind the village. Neighbors who saw her effort would sometimes encourage Tuti, but most laughed or shook their heads.

The Council had not said what particular tasks would be required for Tuti's Fifth Moon examination, so she prepared for all that she could remember from observing past contests. Moytoy, now 17 winters old and Allijay's most accomplished competitor, felt no threat from Tuti, and graciously worked with her on several tests that she had not seen. The months passed slowly, but Tuti felt her body gaining strength as well as speed. This surprised her, for she had thought she was already in shape for any challenge.

∞

Now the testing time was at hand. It was the moon of deep frost and the air and waters were showing a distinct chill. Three Council members, including Sadayi, and two race monitors would be present to set the tasks for Tuti and to judge her performance. Failure to perform any one of the tasks would bar Tuti from the Grand River Run. For convenience, the three tests would be done in the same spot, although in the actual competition they would be set quite apart from each other.

The gray-haired elder's gaze held Tuti in frozen silence. She waited for him to speak, her heart pounding, knowing he was one of the doubters, one who would just as soon have not even given her this opportunity, and had no illusions that she would do anything but fail.

"Your three tests are these, and will be attempted in the order that I give them to you — the tree climb, the fire swim and the deer swim."

"Oh my God," gulped Tuti as her thoughts raced, "You have done your best to assure my failure. Two swim tests across this river in frigid water. The Grand River Run is not held in conditions like these. Why me? Why now?" But she already knew the answer to her thoughts and simply replied, "I'm ready."

"Good. We will proceed. The tree that you will attempt to climb stands ten strides to your left. An owl feather has been placed in the topmost branches. Bring us the owl feather, we will observe, and if you are successful you may move to the next task."

"Yes!" thought Tuti, "I am light, my arms strong and I have climbed almost since I could walk. This I can do, and do well." She leaped to catch a lower branch, swung herself up, and began to climb hand over hand. She was soon near the top. "There it is," she said to herself, "tucked under that flap of bark. I knew it couldn't be out on the weaker branches if a man had to place it there."

Gripping the feather between her teeth, she scurried down almost as quickly as a squirrel. Just before the final leap, a dead branch snapped but Tuti regained her balance quickly, grabbed a second branch, and dropped easily to the ground. She noticed smoke billowing from behind a rock outcropping as she presented the owl feather to the waiting elder.

"The fire is ready. You will run through it, selecting a burning brand from the center of the flames. You must swim the river at this point, keeping the fire alive. When you reach the opposite shore — if you do — you must have flame or ember enough, and start a fire upon the flat rock that you see on the far shore. If you are successful, you will find a deerskin containing ten stones the size of my fist. It is your task to return to this shore with that load, as if you were bringing home the carcass of a deer. Any questions?"

"No. I am well acquainted with these tasks." Even though Tuti wanted to add, "But never have I seen them attempted with ice in the shallows." She stepped around the rocks to where the fire now burned, as the elders watched in silence.

"May I choose well," though Tuti, as she stared into the flames. Then she saw the one she must have, the piece of pine with a burning knot near the end, and with three strides she plowed through the fire and had the branch in her hand. But the whole length of the stick was aflame, searing her skin.

Teeth clenched, she held her grip and plunged into the icy water, keeping the burning knot a foot above the surface. The pain in her hand lessened, but the frigid water seemed to tear all breath from her lungs. Only speed would save her now and she kicked as she never had before. At last she could feel the slippery river bed beneath her numb feet and turned her attention to the torch, which had lost its flame and showed only a faint trail of smoke.

Tuti's hands and feet felt like clubs as she stumbled from the water but quickly she turned her attention to the torch, thrusting the now glowing end into a patch of dry moss. Smoke continued to emerge. She had taken note of the cedar tree from the other side, was there in five shaky strides, drawing her knife from her beaded tunic. In a moment she had shaved a handful of the fuzzy inner bark, turned to the dry and dead lower branches of a nearby pine and rapidly filled her arms with kindling.

Keeping the faint ember wrapped in the moss, Tuti laid it on the low, flat rock and carefully placed the cedar tinder around it. She wasn't sure that she had any breath left after the swim, but holding her face close, managed to blow weakly at the remains of the coal. The ember was dying, and with it, her hopes. There would be no second chance for her next year — this she knew.

Just as she was certain that the task was lost, a small flame leaped through the tinder, kindling another flame of confidence in her heart. The rest was easy as she fed sticks of increasing size into the blaze and soon had a cozy fire burning atop the rock.

Tuti had hoped for a few moments respite to regain some body warmth and strength close to the fire, but caught sight of the impatient countenance of the elder, signaling her to pick up the skin of stones so that she could move into the final test. Her emotions rising in a surge of anger, she kicked the fire into the river.

Muscles aching with cold and fatigue, Tuti could barely lift the weighted skin to her fire rock. She ducked low and transferred the load to her shoulder. "How will I ever make it back myself, let alone dragging a skin of stones?" Tuti pondered, as her eyes scanned the flowing river, which now seemed twice as wide as before, a frigid barrier between herself and the people she loved.

"And suppose I stop moving and the current washes me away, will they stand there and let me drown?" Tuti knew that such an outcome was not likely as one of the two monitors observing her, Kanegwati ("water moccasin"), was known for his swimming ability and appeared to be dressed to enter the water if necessary.

All eyes were on Tuti as she dragged the skin into the shallows and struck out toward the group waiting for her on the far shore. Then she tried to cross the first shoot of rushing water and disappeared. "Get her," said the elder, turning toward Kanegwati, who immediately stripped off his tunic and plunged in.

Tuti surfaced with a gasp for air twenty feet downstream, clinging to a river rock. But the close call seemed to have touched some source of energy deep within her. "Stop! Go back! I still have the skin," she yelled at Kanegwati. Kanegwati did not go back, but neither did he continue toward Tuti, he simply held his position where he could watch her and climbed onto his own rock.

At this point, Tuti realized that she could not complete the river crossing in the same way, but was not about to give up on the test after having come this far. What chance did she have, though? What could make it possible for her to finish? The log! That small log caught on the rock right next to her!! Nothing the elder had told her ruled out a floating aid, particularly one that seemed to appear of its own volition.

Tuti pulled and the log came loose. Lodged where it was out of the river in recent months, it had plenty of buoyancy. She pulled the cords of the skin across the log, wound them around her hand, and then pulled as much of her body out of the water and onto the log as balance would permit. The observers looked at each other and smiled briefly. This kind of innovative thinking would serve any contestant well, and Tuti had certainly demonstrated her resourcefulness today.

Tuti's strong legs were able to kick like the frog, although she pushed ashore fifty paces below the point where she had started and, again, she could not feel her hands and feet. Kanegwati returned to the group, chilled to the bone himself. Tuti glared at that monstrous bag of stones, but gritted her teeth and dragged it to the feet of the elder who had assigned her the tasks. He did not speak or smile, but slowly nodded and turned away.

Another elder had built up the original fire, which was now reflecting its warmth from the rocky wall behind. The monitors and elders turned to leave, only Sadayi and Tuti remaining.

"Oh, my dear one, my dear one! What courage you have shown today. As you know, many gave you no chance at all, but they were wrong. They did not know the strength that you carry inside. Here, my dear, I have brought you dry clothing. I will help you change as the warmth returns to your body."

Sadayi's words warmed Tuti's heart, just as the flames and dry skins were giving comfort to her body. The two sat close to the fire in silence until Tuti stirred and tested each of her limbs in turn. Satisfied that her legs would once again support her, she and Sadayi rose and scattered the remaining coals. Then the pair smiled at each other with deep understanding and headed back to the village.

∞

The last of autumn and then the winter months dragged slowly by. But Tuti did not huddle inside when the weather grew fierce. She might modify her routine, but every spare moment was still spent in increasing her stamina. She would be the one to carry in the hind quarter of venison for their extended family, or to gather firewood in deep snow. As the snow melted away, she would fly down the trails for speed, until laughing neighbors nicknamed her "Breeze That Never Ceases."

Now at last came the moon of large leaf blossoms, the moon before the Grand River Run would be held. The elders of Allijay sent word as far as the villages of Tsatugi on the Chattooga River and Kituhwa on the Tuckasegee River for those people to bring their most outstanding young braves to the annual competition.

Braves?! It was then that Tuti realized that most still assumed that this would be an event for males only, and that her presence was not a certainty in any respect. She had known deep down that, despite her having passed those three tests before the elders, that the five athletes who would represent Allijay must be selected just before the competition.

As soon as word went out to the neighboring villages, the elders of Allijay called their village together around a council fire. "It is time that our own runners are known to all, so that they may prepare and bring honor to Allijay." Tuti listened with a sinking heart as each young brave was named and asked to stand before the assembled village.

Her mind was far away, musing on the difficult tests she had performed last winter, as she gazed at the four figures who proudly stood in the dancing light. Then, with a jolt, she suddenly realized that her own name had just been called. "Oh yes, oh yes!" This was the chance she had been striving to achieve for nearly a year. Tuti smoothed her braids and walked to join the group at the fire. A glance at her family showed the pride glowing in their eyes.

The next fortnight brought a frenzy of activity. The chosen five trained as they never had before. Finishing touches were put on the new townhouse. Food was inventoried, caches opened and hunting parties dispatched to find deer and smaller animals. At last the time was at hand and guests began to arrive, new skin tents rising on the outskirts of the village.

The evening before the race, all competitors were called together and given updated instructions. Two new tasks had been added this year, including the "wounded warrior carry" and the "flaming arrow shoot." There would be monitors at all critical points to keep track of progress, see that tasks were performed properly, and to come to the aid of any competitor in need. A competitor receiving aid, of course, would be out of the race.

∞

The day dawned unseasonably cold for springtime and the river did not appear inviting. Tuti recalled her own frigid qualifying tests and simply smiled inwardly.

Despite their duties as hosts, Tuti's family had all gathered at the race start to give her the encouragement of their presence. Before the competitors took their starting positions, her father had spoken to her alone. "Tuti, you may have guessed, as you and each of your sisters were born, I briefly regretted not having a son. Never again shall I have such a thought. Your spirit towers over my own, and one day you will be a beloved leader of our village." Tuti blinked back tears of gratitude.

Sadayi drew Tuti aside and their eyes met in understanding. "There are some great athletes in this race, but I expect you to do well. However, if you do no more than finish the course, you will have brought great honor to our clan." Tuti smiled her thanks.

The race started at dawn and, as luck would have it, the tree climb was first, only this time there were at least thirty trees with owl feathers in their tops, some with three or four. Tuti knew this was an event where she could shine, and she did exactly that. As she pressed the owl feather into the monitor's hand and leaped back onto the trail, she realized that she must be ahead of at least two-thirds of the competitors. Her arms and legs felt fully alive as she nearly flew along the course, living up to her nickname, Breeze that Never Ceases.

The wounded warrior carry was one of the tougher tasks Tuti encountered. There were plenty of "wounded" volunteers, but no lightweights among them. She rolled the "warrior" onto his back, pushed her head into his side, and then rolled him onto her shoulders. She was barely able to straighten up from her crouch, hook an arm around one leg and grab the opposite wrist with her hand. Then she half ran, half staggered to the small meadow beyond the next bend in the river. "Sorry," she exclaimed, as she dropped the "body" rather abruptly near the next monitor.

One by one, the tasks fell behind her, including the swims, which were much easier in warmer weather and water. Still her legs felt fresh, as if she could run on into the night, and every once in a while she passed a surprised runner. The sun told her that they had reached mid-afternoon as she blew into the deer shoot and snatched up a bow.

Tuksi, one of the hometown monitors, was at this station. Monitors were not to cheer for their own runners, but simply be available as needed. He whispered to Tuti, "That's Moytoy just finishing the shoot over there. He's in first place. This is the last test — you both will make our village so very proud."

Tuti couldn't believe her ears. Was she really in second place? She chose five arrows, kept hand and eye ever so steady, and shot all five into the designated circle on the beech tree fifty paces away. The longest run of the day lay ahead, such a distance that two monitors were necessary to make sure the runners stayed on course.

Time passed, the sun dipped, and still she ran, even though the trail turned up along a set of cliffs, passing another monitor in the process. Now she was down at river level again when she saw a flash of motion far ahead through the trees. Yes, it was Moytoy! She had gained on him, was gaining on him even now.

The trail turned toward the river and Tuti heard a voice. It must be the last monitor. She could see the river's edge through the laurel as sunlight flashed off of the ripples. "HELP! I need help." The young woman, whom Tuti had never seen before, lay beneath a laurel bush, a dark bruise spreading up her right calf. The rattlesnake was coiled near a rock beside the river.

Tuti's mind raced, grasping the situation in an instant. All of her training for the past year was about to go for naught. Yet this woman needed help and needed it now. But Tuti was so close, she might even win the race if she could catch Moytoy. There was enough time to do it and what a triumph for women, for her village, for herself. The next runner, or one even farther back, could surely help. But no, she knew the answer in her heart, choked back her tears and knelt beside the woman.

"I am Awiakta, from the village of Setsi," she whispered. My people brought me with them as a monitor. I went from my station to the river to drink and had just been bitten when you appeared. The snake is still close by. Be careful." Two runners came dashing past. Tuti picked up a branch and hurried the rattlesnake into the river. She knew it would swim and come ashore somewhere downstream.

She pulled Awiakta to a nearby maple where she could sit and keep her heart above the bite. Tuti saw the earthen bowl and filled it with water. "Drink all you can. It will help dilute the poison and move it through your body. Now I need snake plant — but that will be easy." She brought the leaves and root to Awiakta. "Chew on these while I search for comfrey." She knew that would mean finding a clearing with enough sunlight for it to grow at the edge and as she looked for the plant, another dozen runners shot by on the trail.

Luck was with her and Tuti found comfrey in the first clearing she searched. She returned with two dozen leaves and some pipsissawa as well. Gathering cedar tinder and using the bow and spindle from Awiakta's pouch, Tuti soon had a fire going and water heating in the bowl. Probably half the runners had passed by this time.

The comfrey leaves were steaming in the hot water. Tuti took half of them and the thongs from her tunic and bound them over the wound in a hot compress. "Daughter, you have learned well. I did not have to point the way for any of your help, and you may well have saved my life." She smiled at Tuti.

"With the pipsissawa we will make a hot tea and that will help the poison pass even faster than water," Tuti said as she placed the bowl over the fire once more. More runners, some looking exhausted, thundered past.

"My dear," continued Awiakta, "How were you helping with the race? Did I take you from your duties?

It was then that Tuti lost it, as tears welled up in her eyes and she broke into uncontrollable sobbing. "I was in the race," her tiny, choking voice replied. Awiakta looked puzzled.

Just then, Tuti and Awiakta could hear voices from a group of monitors jogging up the trail. As the party neared, they spotted the two women. "All the runners have passed and our duties are over. We can head for the feast." Then Kanegwati recognized Tuti and gave her a questioning look.

Tuti responded to Kanegwati's look with a command, "Take good care of Awiakta and get her back to the village. I must finish the race." And with that, Tuti was down the trail like a deer, tears streaming down her cheeks all the way. As she crossed the finish line three miles later, the elders simply smiled and nodded at her, as if they had known all along that a last place finish would be the outcome.

∞

As in years past, the feast was followed by the fire, where recognition and awards would be given. The winner, Moytoy, who had indeed made Allijay proud, was given a fine new bow, made by Awahili, one of the village's most respected craftsmen. Four more, all from neighboring villages, were cited for their skill in overcoming obstacles, and other stories were told which made the group shake with laughter. Awiakta leaned against a pile of skins, and looked much better than when Tuti had last seen her. But the big event had now come to an end and Tuti felt the mixed emotions and sadness inside herself.

But as the large gathering was about to turn to informal visiting, Saligugi, the doubting elder who had originally set Tuti's tasks, rose to address the crowd. "We have officially recognized the winners of the Grand River Run for their skill and prowess, and this is as it should be. However, something else happened today of which many of you may be unaware.

"Eleven moons ago, Sadayi, the head of our clan and a woman known for her wisdom, came to me telling of the desire of one of our young people to compete in this race — a young woman. I felt that women had no place in this competition and so I said 'no.' I was overruled by the rest of our Council and grudgingly agreed to give her three tests to prove herself able to endure this most difficult race. Let no one ever doubt her endurance again.

"Three persons have spoken with me tonight during the feast, and their stories, taken together, make an astounding tale. Tuksi, as you know, was monitor at the last challenge station. Tuti reached that station just as Moytoy was leaving and there was no doubt that she was in second place at that moment. Tuksi confirmed it. Moytoy himself was aware of Tuti's position and twice looked back, seeing that she was closing the space between them. Could Tuti have caught and passed him? Moytoy thinks it possible, but we will never know the answer to that question.

"This brings us to the most intriguing part of the story. The last monitor, Awiakta, from the village of Setsi, was positioned so that she could guide runners up the river trail portion of the course. She had headed to the river bank to get a drink just after Moytoy passed, when she was bitten by a rattlesnake.

"In great pain and barely able to drag herself back to the trail, she saw Tuti approaching and thought that, being female, she was one of the race helpers. She hailed her as best she could, Tuti stopped, and the rest will become one of our legends. Awiakta is here with us tonight because Tuti gave up her own chance for glory, made good healing medicine and stayed with her until more help arrived."

There was a murmur from the crowd, as many turned and smiled at Tuti. "Wait, there is more!" Saligugi raised his voice over the folks trying to congratulate Tuti. "Never has a last place finisher been more of a winner. I — and I know Awiakta joins me — would like to present this tunic, with its rattlesnake skin sash to Tuti so that she will remember the day when compassion triumphed over personal glory.

"And so that the deeds of this day will be remembered by all in years to come — and the Council has agreed to this in one of the speediest decisions ever — this race will, from this day forward, be known as Tuti's Triumph."

∞ ∞ ∞

The names used in this story — of both places and people — are all traditional, belonging to the Cherokee in the time when they alone inhabited this part of the valley of the Little Tennessee River. The village of Allijay was the heart of this Cherokee community, later known to us as Needmore, situated on what we now know as Licklog Creek.

The basic story was a favorite bedtime tale for our four children, a story that shared a lesson in the contrast between ambition and compassion, and the difficult choices we sometimes have to make in our own lives.

The Bridge of Nevermore
1942

CASSIE'S HEART WAS AS LONELY as if she were watching the last train disappear in the distance, carrying with it her hopes and dreams. Though to be frank, she had never even seen a train, let alone ridden on one. Each day she was surrounded by family, crops and animals as she went about the demanding tasks that mountain farming required, but within her heart she knew that there had to be more.

At sixteen, Cassie was the oldest of four sisters. Her clothing was simple and unflattering, billowing utilitarian dresses that would be passed from sister to sister. But her face was open and honest and when she smiled, her feelings radiated joy to those around her. Her body had already gone through its physical changes into womanhood. These she recognized, but the moods that swept over her at unexpected times were still a mystery.

Her family's farm was nestled within a sweeping elbow of Brush Creek, not far from the spot where the creek waters joined those of the Little Tennessee River. That there was a farm there at all was nothing short of a small miracle. No road, not even a wagon track, approached her family's land — only a foot trail wound its way from the swinging bridge, through the sycamores and laurel on the riverbank, to the farm a mile up river. What little livestock they had, had been brought over in their rowboat, the cow tied to the back of the boat with a rope to swim. Tools and small farm implements had come the same way, or else been wrestled across the narrow bridge by hand.

"Cassie, I need you to churn this cream into butter and divide it while I get jars steamed for the tomato canning," her mother's voice called from the kitchen, where the wood cookstove was throwing out more heat than they needed for warmth. Cassie had milked their one Guernsey cow earlier that morning.

Cassie replied in frustration. "Ma, you know I want to teach school, but I've got to find a way to finish high school first." Cassie had attended the one room Hightower School three miles away, a walk made difficult when the river was running high. But her folks had pulled her out after sixth grade, saying, "The farm work is more important, young lady."

"We've been through this a hundred times, Cassie. High school would mean Bryson City, and we cain't afford to board you there. Now hush, and get to work!" Once again, her heart sank. Beautiful as their land, woods and creek were, it felt as if her world barely existed. She needed more.

Two or three times a month, the family would walk the trail, cross the river on the swinging bridge, and follow the wagon track to the small whitewashed Hightower School that doubled as a church for the scattered community, usually when her father had some business to conduct with someone in the congregation. The preacher always had a scorching message about sin, but in compensation there would be other young people there.

She had seen Adam a half dozen times. He was not a teenager like herself, perhaps in his early twenties, Cassie guessed. Adam and his family had come from Georgia last year and now worked a piece of land above High Lonesome. His smile had seemed to make something jump inside her breast when their eyes met, but they had never had a chance to speak to each other. Even so, she was sure there was a connection between them. But Pa watched her with the eyes of a red-tailed hawk. When Adam inclined his head toward the door, she had had to shake her head and miss the possibility of a word with him.

But this was one of those blue-sky Sundays of winter and Cassie found herself at the little church once again, her family's attention turned toward their neighbors, sharing the tales of hardship which they all endured. Something brushed her hand and she almost jerked it back, but in the next instant fingers were pressing a folded scrap of paper into her hand, footsteps hurrying away.

Heart pounding, she fled to the privy, the only private place where she wouldn't be questioned, and quickly unfolded the paper. The carefully crafted note — undoubtedly written before Adam had left home — read,

> *Will you meet me on the bridge Wednesday night? After dusk has passed? You will know my whistle.*

Hardly able to breathe, she made her way back to the visiting church neighbors. Ma and Pa would never approve, of course. And what about her own conscience? Should she? Could she? Did she have enough courage? It would have to be a secret rendezvous. And a voice inside her kept saying, "Cassie, this is not a wise thing to even consider."

Flushed and shaking, and she felt as if her thoughts were written in the air above her head for all to see. She backed against a wall to catch her breath and calm her nerves. Then she caught Adam's eyes watching her and her knees almost failed her. But for a moment, she held his gaze and nodded ever so slightly.

∞

The moon was full and lit the little farmstead so brilliantly that no lantern was needed to show the path. Silver reflections sparkled from the flowing river. Cassie had waited until her family was asleep and slipped out of the cabin without a sound. She ran her comb through her hair for the third time since leaving. Wrapped in her scarf were fresh biscuits from the afternoon's baking and her eager feet skipped down the path. The bridge was in sight.

She climbed carefully up the several steps at the end of the bridge and stepped onto the gently swaying planks and cables. Moonlight caught in her hair and the folds of her dress as a light breeze followed her above the water.

Would Adam be here too? She was sure he would, but for a moment, fear and doubt told her she was alone. Suppose she had misread the note, he had waited, given up and already left? Perhaps he had meant a different night. Or was this not Wednesday?

A horse whinnied on the far bank and her heart leaped. Then she heard it — the sound she had longed for — so close that it gave her a start. The distinctive whistle of the whip-poor-will, where no whip-poor-will should be calling at this time of year. Without a thought, she gave a bob-white whistle in return. And waited.

The whip-poor-will called again and suddenly they were running toward each other on the swaying bridge, as if a magnet were pulling at their hearts. In the center of the bridge, an arm's length from each other, they stopped. Gently they touched hands, and their fingers interlaced for a moment before drawing away. "You came!" they both exclaimed with the same voice, then laughed and looked away.

"How long can you stay?" Adam asked.

Cassie thought of her folks, always up before the sun. If they missed her, she would never be able to meet Adam again. "I'll tell you when I must go, but for now the night is ours."

"Oh no! What have I just said?" Cassie thought to herself. "How could I be so bold?" Had her unpredictable feelings thrown any trace of good judgment into the river? What did Adam think of those words?

"The island," Adam was saying. "I'll climb down first and then catch you when you jump." The river was so wide at this point that the bridge, although it appeared to be continuous, was actually two spans joining at a timber pier on a half-mile long island. It was not likely that anyone would be passing by on the trails at this hour, but even so, the island would be a secluded spot where they could talk.

His arms felt to Cassie as if they could lift her whole world as he swung her easily down from the bridge. They walked upriver through the trees, Black Saint's blanket looped over Adam's shoulder, until they found a grassy moonlit clearing near the water's edge. Here Adam spread the blanket for them to sit and boldly pulled Cassie close to his side, her head resting on his shoulder.

The fluttering in her breast, a new but delightful feeling for Cassie, made her only snuggle closer. Adam's coveralls were filled with the rich scent of horses and plowed earth.

"Are you hungry?" Cassie asked as she unwrapped the biscuits and offered them to Adam. "I should have brought honey, too."

"Delicious!" Adam's compliment was genuine as he took a bite from one, even though the fullness of each other's presence drove all thought of food from their minds.

They spoke of many things, but mostly of their lives, their dreams, the frustrations and contradictions of their present family life. Floodgates of the soul had opened. The closeness, not just of body, but of their spirits, was palpable. Cassie yearned to be a teacher, but felt that Ma and Pa would keep her on the farmstead until she herself became an old lady.

Adam knew that his life was about to take a very different direction. The whole country was in shock from the Japanese bombardment of the U.S. Naval Fleet at Pearl Harbor last month and young men were rushing to join the military. However, construction of a dam on the Little Tennessee River, vital to the war effort, had started a week ago and capable workers were urgently needed. It was a choice that Adam would have to make very soon.

The moon, which had been high overhead at their meeting on the bridge, was now sinking to the ridge top in the west. For a time they lay in silence, listening to the murmuring voice of the river, drawn close in a lovers' embrace, snuggled beneath Adam's coat. All cares were suspended in time as their lips met and their hands explored each other's bodies.

They wanted each other passionately and equally, and there was no turning back. Their night was full of exploding rainbows and the young lovers went where neither of them had gone before. Past mysteries were now revealed. Once more they drew each other close, pulled Adam's coat and Cassie's shawl over their shivering skin, and dozed for a time.

An owl's plaintive call startled them both. "Oh! Oh! Oh! It's almost dawn," sobbed Cassie. "What will I do? What will I say? What can I say?" They dressed, racing against the dawn, and climbed to the bridge. "Oh Adam, will I see you here again? I must! I must!"

"Yes! Yes, my love. I know you have to run — and Black Saint is restless and hungry. We will meet at the bridge again. A note at church and, if not, I will leave a note under the last plank on your side of the bridge whenever I come this way. If you can, leave me a note in the same place."

Over the bridge and down the path, Cassie's feet flew as they had never done before. She was out of sight before Black Saint's hoof beats echoed across the water.

Cassie slowed to catch her breath as the milking shed came into view. "Just let me get to the chicken yard and start collecting eggs before anyone sees me," she thought. She pulled the door open and reached for the basket, then nearly jumped out of her skin when a voice behind her demanded, "Tell me just where you have been, you sinful child, and don't tell me you came out for early chores, because I've been here since first light!"

Cassie gulped as the blood rushed to her face and she groped for some kind of reply. "Pa, it was so beautiful and mild that I took an early morning walk by the river. Did you hear the owl?"

"I don't believe you. Maybe this belt on your behind will make you remember. Now get to work this instant and you are not to be out of the cabin or out of my sight or Ma's until I tell you. And that won't be for a long time."

∞

Cassie's backside stung and it was hard to hold back her tears, but her heart ached even more. Not only was she under the constant observation of her parents, the house locked at night, but she was not allowed to go to church on the Sundays when the rest of the family went. When the others made the church trip, Cassie and her three-year-old sister, Sadie, were left behind.

But this arrangement had one advantage — the two sisters always took a Sunday walk to the swinging bridge, where Cassie would find Adam's notes and leave one of her own. This was not easy, as she would have to distract Sadie with stick boats dropped from the bridge, while she found Adam's note, or hid her own. The weeks went by, and became months, Cassie feeling as if she were in prison.

By now, Adam knew her situation, and the reason she could not appear at the bridge. So it was, one Sunday morning, that Cassie wrote her note of desperation.

> *Adam, I think I am with child — our child, of course. We must leave. You spoke of work to the west, where dams will be built and times may be better than they are now. Meet me at the bridge Friday night — I can't give you a time, but it will be after dark and I will find a way somehow — we will ride — ride together. I will bring only a bit of extra clothing. This should be time enough for you to find this note, though I will not be able to get yours. I love you, Cassie*

It was a rare Monday that Adam did not check for Cassie's "Sunday note" on his way to the mica mine where he worked three days a week, and this Monday was no exception. Color spread to his face as he read and reread the words, glad that there was no one close by to question him. He would meet her Friday night, of that he had no doubt. But the hurt that it would cause his family troubled him deeply.

For Cassie, the five days from Sunday to Friday seemed like a year. She prayed that Adam would get the note — and that he could do as she asked. What a demand to make of anyone, even best friend or husband. And she had one more task — writing a note to her family, telling them that she loved them dearly, but she must go — not why or where or with whom — but simply that her own life must be somewhere with more opportunity. She imagined Adam writing a similar note to his family.

Friday came, and with it a spring storm. "Good, thought Cassie, the rain and thunder will provide cover for what I need to do." She had already carefully rolled her travel clothing into a small bundle, along with her treasured comb and small lump of homemade soap, and tucked the bundle in beside her pillow. She had been planning her escape from the house all week, loosening the window in the room where she and her sisters slept, and rubbing lard on the frame, so that it wouldn't squeak when opened.

∞

It was a long ride from High Lonesome down to the swinging bridge, and Adam wanted to keep Black Saint as rested as possible, not knowing whether he and Cassie would be pursued that night. Adam had left his family note under the water dipper, where he knew it would be found in the morning when his mother filled the pitchers, saying simply that he had gone to help his country

He quietly led Black Saint on foot until they were well clear of the last split rail fence, then swung his lean body into the saddle. The rain that had been relentless all day, was beginning to slacken as dusk enveloped the horse and rider, though the trail was muddy and treacherous.

Now he was at the river, startled by what he could see of the rushing water, but confident that the bridge, five miles away, would hold. Darkness closed in and he had to trust his mount more than ever on the narrow trail. They were splashing through Rattlesnake Creek, now Licklog, and there was river water covering the trail in places. But he was close — very close.

∞

Cassie did her chores, and a few for her sisters, with enthusiasm that day, even though she had to dodge running water and puddles as she dashed through the pounding rain. She helped cook and clean up, as usual, but gave Ma an extra warm hug after dinner.

She dutifully listened as her Pa read from the Good Book, something about "the wages of sin being death." His words and tone of voice gave her the shivers. Cassie climbed into bed, still wearing her clothes, and listened to the breathing of her younger sisters.

Finally satisfied that they were genuinely asleep, Cassie looked to the window, then to the locked front door where the lantern hung. Her Pa now slept with the key. She planned to borrow the family lantern and leave it at the bridge, for there was no way to see the trail on so dark a night with the thick cloud cover. But first she would toss her clothing bundle out of the window and then go for the lantern.

When the bundle hit, it landed on a small branch that the storm had knocked loose, cracking it like a footstep. Barley, the old redbone hound, thinking that an intruder was much too close to the house, came baying around the side of the cabin.

Cassie heard her Pa's feet hit the floor and, forgoing the lantern, she dropped over the window sill, giving Barley a hug to quiet him. Quickly she scooped up her wet and muddy travel bundle, ran toward the creek and crouched behind some laurel to see what her Pa would do.

It took him a few minutes to light the lantern, grab his rifle and get the door unlocked. He circled the cabin carefully and saw Cassie's open window. She heard him curse. Pa ran back inside to make sure she was gone, then took off down the trail as if chased by demons. He was quickly out of sight, so Cassie never saw him slip and fall, or the lantern shatter on a rock. He couldn't see and his knee would hardly support him — retreat was the only option. Pa snatched up the muddy rifle and slowly felt his way as he crawled back up the trail.

Meanwhile, Cassie's mind was racing and her heart was in her throat. She had no light and Pa was between her and Adam. It had all come down to this night, this moment. She had to get to Adam somehow. "Oh, Cassie," she thought, "No tears yet. Think! You've got to think of a way."

Her thoughts went tumbling over each other, then paused. She looked into the darkness with a shiver. "Of course. The boat. I should have thought of it before." The water was high — she had seen it rising all day — but there was no rough water between here and the bridge. She could tie the boat off at the bridge steps and her Pa would find it later.

The path to where the boat was kept farther down the creek was familiar, even in the dark, and Cassie was soon there, placing her bundle on the seat, untying the rope, and pushing off with an oar. The oar was long and awkward, but she would use it like a paddle, trying to keep the boat on course.

It took only a few minutes before Cassie and the little boat reached the mouth of the creek and spun into the river in the dark. In an instant, her whole world changed. She could feel the boat toss, and water splashed over the sides. "My God!" thought Cassie, "There are no waves in this part of the river." But tonight there were. "Oh Adam! Please be there!"

In the dark, how would she know she was at the bridge? How would she stop? Could she stop? Her mind raced and the boat fairly flew through the blackness.

"What is that roar? That tiny ledge above the bridge couldn't be making that sound, could it?" The boat lurched as it hit the watery hole, then rose on its stern, and rolled to one side, dumping Cassie and her oar into the raging flow.

"Adam!!" she screamed, just as the muddy water closed over her face and choked off more cries. She surfaced once more, thinking that she heard the whip-poor-will call from the far shore through the roar of the river. The dreams that had given her the courage to come this far were drowning in the dark and cold of the angry river. Her strength and spirit seemed to have fled.

∞

Pa's boat was found by Cole Hyatt two days later, smashed and hung on the rocks below Sawmill Creek. Cassie's pitiful bundle of clothes, caught on a snag, was retrieved with a sob by her sister Sadie when the water had finally receded enough to reveal it. Though the neighbors in the valley searched the river for weeks, Cassie's body was never found.

∞ ∞ ∞

Cassie's farm is a very real place, situated exactly as I have described it. In the time of Needmore, when it was a thriving community, it was known as the Hampton Farm. As a family, we have walked to it many times, often with friends, crossing the swinging bridge at Needmore to reach it.

There is another swinging bridge at Sawmill Creek and one upstream in Oak Grove. These bridges have spanned the river for decades, reminders of the time when this country was penetrated by trails more so than roads, and access was not easy. The Needmore Bridge does require two spans, as you can see in the photo below, meeting at the downstream tip of a mid-river island.

Her cabin never had electricity, even into the 21st century, and the most beautiful spring you ever have drunk from trickles out of the hill into a natural sandstone basin right behind the spot where the cabin once stood. I say "once stood" because, though it was still there a decade ago when the Land Trust for the Little Tennessee acquired the farm, the cabin was intentionally burned when the property was transferred to NC Wildlife Resources Commission. All that stands today is the cabin's stone chimney and the ruins of the small log barn.

But is that the end of Cassie and Adam's story? "What the hell, Mr. Author? Do you have no heart? How could you do her in? And what happened to Adam?"

"Wait a minute. Don't push me into the river! There's another piece of the story you might like to hear!"

∞ ∞ ∞

We all know of the huge dams that were built in the '30s and '40s — Calderwood, Nantahala and, of course, Fontana. During those construction years, an occasional traveler would pass through Needmore on his way back east. One such sojourner, a young man by the name of Bart had worked with the river diversion crew at the Fontana dam.

Yes, he had known a fellow worker by the name of Adam, who could very likely be the missing Needmore youth.

But what really electrified the Needmore settlement was the story Adam had told to Bart late one night by candlelight in Adam's tiny Fontana cabin. Bart knew Adam was married, or at least lived with a woman, and her infant daughter. The woman and child appeared to be asleep, or else didn't wish to be seen. "Where did you find a woman in this lonely mountain work town, where unattached females hardly exist?" Bart asked.

"By the grace of God, as we faced death, we came here together," Adam answered. Then he went on to tell of the near heartbreak of that fateful night. How he had known Cassie was in the river when he heard her scream his name. How he had whistled and whistled to give her hope and galloped Black Saint through the dark to a spot opposite the next river island, just below the bridge. How, at that anxious moment, clouds had blown clear of the moon, illuminating a fearful river scene.

He had known that Cassie was no weakling, and that she could swim, though most in the settlement could not and were terrified of the river currents, even at normal water levels. Adam had caught a glimpse of her in the moonlight, as she was swept under the bridge by the rampaging river, and saw an arm move as if she were trying to pull herself toward the island. Without another moment for thought, he plunged into the river on Black Saint, swimming amid the swirling debris, all the while being carried past the near side of the island. Cassie had disappeared from sight.

The clouds snatched away the light once more, but Adam could feel that the currents he and Black Saint had been fighting had suddenly eased. They had reached the eddy at the downstream tip of the island. "Cassie," he shouted again and again, as there was no longer any need for caution. The only reply was the constant roar from the river.

Once more the moonlight broke through and Adam's heart leaped as he caught a glimpse of the slight figure lying in the shallows, a hand tightly clutching a branch of firmly rooted laurel. He was out of the wet saddle and at Cassie's side in an instant. Her voice was barely audible as she whispered, "Adam, is it really you?"

His reply was simply to gather her limp form into his arms and climb onto Black Saint's back once more. "I'll hold you in front and keep you from falling," Adam murmured into her ear. "Black Saint will know the best way to get free of the river." Once more they plunged into the cold waters rushing through the night and were nearly swept around the bend and away from the trail.

But Black Saint had strength and sense enough to gain the bank in time, and together the three of them stumbled up to the trail. "My clothes are torn and soaked," gasped Cassie, "and the travel food and extra clothing are somewhere in the river. I'm so cold. But we made it! Oh my God, we made it!"

"Yes love, I think we did." For a long time, all they could do was embrace. "There's tea in my canteen that may have some warmth yet, and a little deer jerky in my saddlebag. Here! The blankets rolled behind the saddle are wet, of course, but being wool they'll still keep you warm. We can't chance staying the night here, so wrap yourself in these and hold tight to my back. We must be well beyond the Nantahala by dawn."

It was a story that Adam had never told to anyone before, but one that would be repeated again and again among the excited residents of Needmore. Cassie and Adam lived!

Joy eventually overcame the hurt and bitterness surrounding their mysterious flight, and little by little, Cassie, Adam and their daughter again became part of the Needmore Community.

∞ ∞ ∞

I must add one more personal note. Even though this is a story con-structed in my imagination, the farm, creek, bridge and river are real places. However, the terrifying river capsize and swim also have a parallel tale within our own family.

In 1980, my two older children, Cricket — 17, David — 15, my wife-to-be, Trish, and I were kayaking the Tatshenshini River in Canada's Yukon Territory for ten days. In the dangerous canyon of the hugely rain-swollen river, we lost three of our four kayaks and much of our food and personal gear. We were separated from each other for many hours. How we survived is a tale in itself, told in the book, *Wherever Waters Flow*.

And lastly, a big thanks to the descendants of Doyle Hampton for letting Cassie and Adam cavort on your family's home place!

A Cry in the Mist
1956

TSALINA AND HER FAMILY lived about as far back as you could go. North Carolina's Snowbird Mountains were wild country — particularly in the mid-fifties — and the tiny rented cabin at the end of the rutted dirt road rarely saw a visitor. Tsalina's two older brothers, Raven and Night Sky, yearned for a more social atmosphere, but to six-year-old Tsalina it was a wonderland of discovery.

Each season painted a new panorama — the broad brush of delicate, emerging springtime greens; the lush foliage of summer in a wild country full of leaping creeks; the muted oaks, brilliant hickory and striking maple of autumn; and winter's mantle of snow, renewing the natural world once more.

But Tsalina had the sharp eyes of her people, who had lived in these mountains for centuries before the whites arrived. She could find her way in the thickest mist, be the first to see the scarlet seed of "hearts-a-bustin'" when it cracked its prickly shell in the fall, and could spot the motionless copperhead by the subtle difference in pattern between its skin and the surrounding leaves.

Her parents, Sunrise and Tall Bear, met when they were both eighteen, living on the Qualla Boundary, the piece of land, at last — almost four decades later — set aside by an act of the U.S. Congress for the Cherokee who had escaped the 1838 Trail of Tears and hidden in North Carolina's Snowbirds. Tsali, who had given his life that his people might remain, was a distant cousin of Sunrise, and a revered ancestor for whom Tsalina had been named.

Tsalina's father, Tall Bear, had served as a medic in the U.S. Navy for the last two years of World War II aboard the USS *Twiggs*, a destroyer operating in the Pacific. His exceptional strength, and his devotion to healing, had been a source of inspiration to his shipmates. His left leg had been lacerated by flying shrapnel when his ship had been hit by kamikaze aircraft off Okinawa in June of 1945, but he had managed to pull a buddy from a burning gun turret and get them both into a life raft before the *Twiggs* went down in a series of explosions.

However, coming home had been a shock. Gone was the camaraderie of working together on the ship and trusting his very life to his buddy's judgment. Movies still showed the Indians as the "bad guys;" audiences cheering when the cavalry rode over the hill to rescue the wagon train. The term "Native American" did not yet exist. Dee Brown's *Bury My Heart at Wounded Knee*, gradually prodding a nation's consciousness, would not appear until 1970. The FBI's scrutiny — even persecution, many would say — of the American Indian Movement would bring government injustice into sharp national focus with the occupation of Wounded Knee and the trial of Leonard Peltier, but that would not happen for another two decades.

Sunrise was already pregnant when Tall Bear left for his Navy duty. Raven was born in the Qualla home of Sunrise's parents while the *Twiggs* was steaming for Okinawa. When Tall Bear returned at twenty, after his injury and survival at sea, the pair decided to make their home in the Snowbirds, wild country that had always held a mystical, almost magnetic attraction for them. It was here that Night Sky entered their world, and four years later, Tsalina, both with the assistance of an elderly Cherokee midwife who came to live in their dilapidated rented cabin for the last week of each pregnancy.

Life in their tiny cabin with its packed dirt floor presented difficulties that only made their poverty more apparent. Living so remotely — with just a handful of neighbors scattered along their road — was what they sought, but it came with disadvantages. There was no hospital within sixty miles, where Tall Bear might have practiced the medical skills he had acquired in the Navy.

Yes, the Parrett Clinic was in Milltown, run by a husband-and-wife doctor team, but because of local prejudice against his people, Tall Bear was not likely to be employed there, veteran or not. He was continually worried that his meager and erratic income from Jordan Construction would be too little to pay their cabin rent.

Although the boys were tough, walking to a spot within range of the school bus was beyond practical limits, particularly in the winter. So a vehicle was necessary, in this case a '38 Chevy pickup truck, always in need of tender care and cobbled-up maintenance, to get the boys to the nearest pickup point for the bus to the Indian School in Snowbird. The truck was also vital to the meager family income, determined by the odd jobs Tall Bear could get in or near the small town of Robbinsville when he wasn't working for Jordan.

Tsalina, however, was not yet in school and had a penchant for exploring the country around their cabin, whether a wild forest or a neighboring farm. Sunrise had given her limits, but Tsalina was always ignoring them, and seemed to have great confidence in her ability to explore, yet find her way home. But her social interactions did not always have the best of outcomes.

One Saturday afternoon she burst through the door of her tiny cabin in tears. "The kids down the road called me an ugly, stupid redskin and one boy threw a rock at me. They told me to 'git home to my shack and don't come back.' I only wanted to be friends with them. I'm not ugly am I, Mom?"

Sunrise gathered her into her arms, thinking of similar incidents in her own life, and assured her of how loved she was. "Lina, you could not be more beautiful, and you're just in time. You can help me make bread for dinner. The woodstove is hot and you can slip the loaf into the little top oven as soon as we finish kneading the dough." Gradually Tsalina's sobs subsided.

But silently Sunrise's emotions welled up and seemed to catch in her throat, "If only we could afford a few yards of dress material, I could sew a new frock and get Lina out of that sack dress. But we have little enough to eat as it is — no bottomland for a crop and only a tiny garden spot near the creek.

∞

Tsalina loved to sing, particularly when she was by herself in the woods, but she could never explain where the words and melodies had come from. "They've always been in my head," she would tell her family. And rather than being frightened by her human presence, songbirds would often come closer and follow her on her forays on the mountain. When Sunrise felt Tsalina had been gone too long, she would step outside and, surely as with a compass, locate her daughter by that small distant voice.

One cool, breezy afternoon Tsalina had been exploring longer than usual and her mother was becoming concerned, since she had not heard the distant singing in well over an hour. But just as Tall Bear and the boys climbed out of the truck, Tsalina streaked out of the woods with obvious excitement. "You'll never guess what I found today! Way up the mountain! Near a falls on the creek! A medicine wheel!!"

Her dad and brothers gathered around while her mother stood by the woodstove, flipping the trout that were frying in the heavy cast iron pan. Tsalina had their full attention. "It was overgrown with ferns, but the rocks were beautiful, a shiny white color. Large stones marked the four directions, and of course I know the other three — Mother Earth, Father Sky and the Spirit that dwells within me.

And I know that spot — it's exactly as grandmother described it with the ancestor trees — it's near where *her* grandmother's family once lived before our people were driven from these mountains! Grandmother, last year when she was still alive, said that our ancestors' spirits still come there in times of great need." Tsalina paused to catch her breath.

Dad was excited too, but cautious. "Tell us where the place is, Lina. Which creek flows nearby?" As familiar as Tsalina was with every ridge, each clear spring and the few ancient oaks that still stood, she had no trouble pinpointing the location of the medicine wheel.

But her dad's face had taken on a serious look. "That's Panther Creek and it's on Old Man Sullivan's land. You've no business there, and I hate to think what would happen if he caught you trespassing. Remember the boys who tried to put a snake in his mailbox last summer? He fired his shotgun over their heads, but nobody was sure whether he meant to miss or not."

They all fell silent.

Old Man Sullivan's family might have been the first whites to live back in this cove. No one really knew, nor did they know him. His cabin looked almost as run down as Sunrise and Tall Bear's rented one. A few chickens scratched around the small barn. Rats had scoured the old corncrib bare.

But Sullivan had a fair piece of bottomland where Panther Creek entered the valley. He raised a couple of acres of tobacco for a cash crop and plowed with his mule pulling the blade while he put his weight to the handles. His garden produced enough potatoes and turnips to see him through the winter. As far as anyone could recall, there had never been a visitor to the old man's place.

Sullivan had lived alone beyond anyone's memory. He might have been ninety; he might have been a hundred and five. His weathered and wrinkled face seemed to hold no discernible expression; tattered coveralls, undershirt and stained felt hat seemed to comprise his whole wardrobe.

When he traveled to town, which was about once every two or three months, it was on the back of his mangy mule. He would hand Hargrave at the Snowbird General Store in Milltown a scrap of paper with the items he needed scrawled on it, count out the cash due, and head over to Tilley, the blacksmith, or down the street to Halley's Hardware. No words were ever spoken.

"They say he's lived by himself so long, he can't talk," volunteered Raven.

"He can talk," piped up Tsalina.

They all stared with amazement at the small, sweet-voiced oracle. The trout sizzled in the pan. Fireflies left silent streaks of light between the window and the woods.

Sunrise finally found her voice, "Just how, my little bird, do *you* know that the old man can speak?

"I took him a bunch of spring wildflowers last week."

"You did *what*? And what happened? Did he chase you or threaten you?"

"No, but he asked me my name. And what's more, he asked how to spell it, so I know he can write, too."

"I don't like it," her father responded. "I don't want you setting foot on his property again, Lina. It's just not smart."

Tsalina was silent, her gaze turned toward the floor. From her body language, they could tell that she didn't agree with her dad's judgment.

But she was noticeably more conscientious in the weeks that followed, careful always to end her exploring and return to the cabin well before dinner time. Sunrise was tuned to Tsalina's distant songs in the forest, as they rose and fell, often disappearing for periods long enough to make Mom uneasy. But she always materialized before the concern grew, usually with berries or wild shoots to make the evening meal tastier.

She would take with her for lunch something that Sunrise had baked that morning or the evening before. Her mom sometimes wondered about her increased appetite, but ultimately passed it off to a growth spurt in her daughter.

Summer faded into autumn, the mountain nights turned cold and morning would often reveal a carpet of frost in the bottomland. The family drew closer to the warmth of the woodstove. Next fall, Tsalina would be starting school at the BIA Indian School and Sunrise could already feel the emptiness gnawing at her heart.

The days were noticeably shorter, the whippoorwills almost silent, and it was now quite dark by dinnertime. Tall Bear and the boys piled out of the truck one October evening to find Sunrise nearly frantic.

"Did you see any sign of Lina on your way in? She hasn't returned from the woods. It's been four or five hours since I heard her song, and now the valley is filled with heavy mist. She's never done this before and I have an awful feeling about it."

"Let's go," responded Tall Bear without hesitation, "Dinner will have to wait. Sunny, I know you want to come too, but someone needs to stay here in case Lina comes home while we're searching." Sunrise blinked back her tears, knowing that she was in for another period of uncertainty while the men were scouring the mountain.

Tall Bear grabbed a flashlight from the truck and Raven found one in the cabin. Night Sky followed with the kerosene lantern. Sunrise was left with a pair of candles as she covered their dinner to hold what warmth might remain.

"Boys, do you think we can find the medicine wheel in this fog and at night? I think we should try that spot first." Tall Bear stuffed some apples and clothing into a rucksack and gave Sunrise a quick hug.

"Be careful, Bear," she murmured into his sweat-stained shirt.

As they stepped over the well-worn door sill, a great horned owl, so close that it made them jump, let loose her plaintive call. No one spoke about the eerie death legend which many of their people connect with the call of an owl. Sunrise stood in the doorway, biting her lip to hold back the tears as she watched her men disappear into the mist.

"I think we should cross the spur, head up the draw and over the next ridge, hitting Panther Creek well above Sullivan's cabin," volunteered Raven.

"That sounds like a good plan," his dad replied.

They had trudged generally upward for over half an hour when Night Sky, breathing hard, said, "We must be close enough to be heard at the medicine wheel by now. Do we take a chance calling for Lina if Sullivan might hear us down at his cabin?"

"I think we have to," replied Tall Bear. Together, they let out a chorus of shouts, then silently waited for a reply.

The piercing response that came through the night mist chilled them to their marrow.

"Aiyee! It is the death song!" murmured Night Sky.

The female keening continued, rising and falling, wrapping itself around their very spirits. "I think we know where the medicine wheel is now," whispered Tall Bear, "but I hate to think what the meaning of what we have just heard may be, for it is indeed the death song."

They wound their way onward, following the sound, until they at last stumbled through Panther Creek. The spirit-like keening had ceased.

With ten minutes of searching, they found the level spot and intricate pattern of stones that marked the sacred site. Tall Bear cautioned them to stay where they were while he searched for signs that Tsalina had been here. He could find none. Nor was there any clue as to the source of the eerie voice which they had all heard.

"Where now?" whispered Night Sky, as they pondered their next move. They had been so sure that the medicine wheel would give them a clue — but now they seemed to have lost direction.

"As risky as a daylight approach might be, going there tonight is ten times worse," replied Tall Bear, "but I think we have no choice. We'll follow the creek down to Old Man Sullivan's cabin. Quietly." He held a finger to his lips.

After half an hour of bushwhacking through laurel and catbriars, they picked up a faint trail by the creek, and in another fifteen minutes could make out the shape of the old man's out-buildings looming through the night mist. Roosting chickens shifted and murmured in one shed as they passed. Thankfully, Sullivan now had no dog to sound the alarm. His old Plott hound had died last winter and he felt no need to replace him.

Darkening the flashlights and turning the lantern low, the trio crept around to the front porch. "Stay here and stay down," whispered Tall Bear. "Let me be the one to knock." He rapped softly and called "Lucas" in a low voice. There was no answer, even with several repetitions.

He started to try the door, then noticed that the latch string had been pulled inside so that the bar could not be raised. Tall Bear edged his way to the window and peered inside. No lamp was lit. He switched on his flashlight and quickly swept the room. His heart leaped into his throat as he saw his daughter in Lucas' lap, the old man's arms loosely around her. Tsalina's eyes were closed and her head lay against his chest as they shared his rocking chair.

"Boys!" he called, moving back to the door, where a strong kick took it right off its old leather hinges and sent it crashing to the floor. There was a small cry as Tsalina opened her eyes. "Daddy, quiet, you're going to wake Luke up!" Tall Bear rushed over to gather her into his arms and make sure she was still in one piece, wondering how his daughter had learned the familiar version of the old man's given name. Sullivan hadn't moved.

"He isn't going to wake up," declared Raven, as he felt for a pulse, first in the old man's wrist, then at his collar bone. There was the faintest smile on Sullivan's face, the first they had ever seen.

"We'll talk to the police and county coroner, but it may be up to us as neighbors to do what has to be done," said Tall Bear. "Right now, we need to get Lina back to Mom as quickly as we can."

"Luke's a nice man," declared Tsalina, not yet realizing that she would never hear his voice again. Tall Bear's thoughts raced as he wondered how many times his daughter had visited the old recluse in secret against his wishes, but he said nothing. He and the boys lifted the body from the chair and gently stretched it out on his bunk. It was still warm.

"Let's set the door back in place and get Lina home." It was then that his eye was drawn to the two biscuits sitting on the table. Without asking Tsalina, he knew that they had been baked by Sunrise yesterday, and brought to Lucas as a gift by his daughter. But, beside the biscuits, was a folded piece of paper, held down by a small stone.

Tall Bear stepped over to the table and unfolded the piece of paper. His jaw dropped and tears came unbidden to his eyes as he read the simple words.

My little time left. Don't have much things. Family all dead. What left is mountain and a little bottom. But is mine. When I die, I give all to Tsalina Walkingstick. Who is my friend.

Lucas B. Sullivan 21 October 1956

Born 11 May 1858 at Little Snowbird

Witness — A. J. Hargrave 21 Oct 1956
L. G. Tilley 10/21/56

∞

It is not hard to imagine the joy in that small family as hugs were exchanged and tears flowed freely with the return of Tsalina and the men. Sunrise wept openly as she set soup and cornbread on the small table, listening to the answers as dozens of questions overflowed her heart.

The conversation, of course, turned often to Lucas Sullivan, how wrongly they had judged him — all except Tsalina — and the great gift he had bestowed upon his young and innocent friend. A gift that would benefit them all in the years to come.

The entire family returned that night to keep watch over Luke's body and at first light, Tall Bear took the old truck, dropped the boys at school and went straight to the courthouse in Robbinsville. The county coroner was sent to confirm the manner of death, calling it failure of the heart. After carefully washing the old man's body and dressing him in the cleanest clothes that they could find, they buried him on a small knoll behind his cabin.

A coffin had been made from boards that the family had collected for their own cabin repairs — a precious pile of lumber that was willingly dedicated to Lucas and his last resting place. Tsalina insisted on building the grave marker — a cairn of mountain rock — some of which she carried, others that she could only roll up from the creek. Come spring, she would plant wildflowers around the cairn.

∞

The Winter Solstice and Christmas were always times of being thankful for life, making it through another year, and for simple homemade gifts to each other in the family. This year, as this special time approached, and they expressed thanks to Lucas Sullivan, Tsalina had an unusual request.

"I want no gifts, as lovingly as you have always crafted them, but I have a request to make of the family."

"You have books here, Mother, and there are some in Luke's cabin. Will you teach me here at home, rather than sending me to the Indian School, where I hear from Raven and Night Sky that they are trying to turn us into proper white citizens and have our culture be forgotten? You and Father both have so much knowledge of our traditional ways. I want to learn all that I can, both of the world outside our cove, and from the experience and understanding of you and our tribal elders. From what Raven and Night Sky tell me about the BIA school, I will not learn what I need at that place.

"Well, that's a surprise, Lina," replied Sunrise. "I know that you are already reading chapter books. Your Father and I will have to talk about this before giving you an answer."

∞

When Sunrise and Tall Bear at last had a few moments to themselves that evening, Tsalina's question was the first topic to tumble out.

"I have no doubt that Tsalina could do this," Sunrise quietly spoke from her pillow. "She is able to read already and she knows the land that surrounds us better than you or I. But what about the law, Bear? Will we be breaking it by keeping her here at home?"

"I think we would, Sunny. It's unusual, but not without precedent. I've heard of a family near Looking Glass Rock schooling their twin daughters themselves, girls that are twelve or thirteen years old. I say we give Lina a chance, have her keep journals of her discoveries, a record of books she reads and notes on the projects she creates. As you just said, her knowledge is already far beyond her years."

"Yes, even though she's quite capable of surprising us — even shocking us — at times, the last thing I want to do is stifle her creativity and enthusiasm. Let's tell her 'yes' and try it out before school is due to start, Bear!"

∞

It was late in the winter when the family learned that the Register of Deeds had searched the Graham County records, determined that Lucas Sullivan had no living relatives, and had been the sole owner of 55 acres of mountain land on Panther Creek.

Although they had not dared to jump to a conclusion, this outcome had been their hope as they trudged back and forth through the snows of an Appalachian mountain winter to feed Lucas' chickens and mule, clean his cabin, and make repairs where necessary.

Tsalina was now the owner of a hardscrabble mountain farm, with its inherent hardships, yet a place that was indeed her own. The court expected her parents, of course, to oversee the functions of the farm, payment of taxes and care of the land until Tsalina reached the age of adulthood.

The clear deed was cause for celebration — a special dinner, many family hugs and an evening for looking ahead. The family would start serious work immediately, as work schedules allowed, planning their use of the new space and making improvements as only your own property will allow. They would be living rent-free and mortgage-free by the end of the following month.

$$\infty$$

Tsalina was never one to wait, however. She immediately staked out her study and collection area in front of the window that caught the first rays of sunshine and a view of Panther Creek. Of all her family members, she was the one to most thoroughly explore Lucas' cabin, as well as the land outside. Small peculiarities, such as a tax bill for the property, paid in cash, a few pieces of women's clothing carefully wrapped in oilskin, and a Christmas angel staring from a dark corner and covered with cobwebs, all tugged at Tsalina's curiosity. "Could Luke once have lived here with his wife or mother," she wondered.

The young girl had just returned to Lucas' cabin from taking the first bouquet of spring flowers to his grave. The fireplace had cooled from the fire built the day before to provide comfort as the family worked to renovate the cabin. Tsalina's hands worked quickly as she tested each stone in the rough hearth. Sure enough, one moved as she wiggled it.

"I knew it!" she exclaimed. "I just knew there was something under it!" The flat stone was heavy, but Tsalina at last raised an edge and rolled it to the side. In the cavity below, surrounded by soil, lay a small metal box with hinges so rusty that they barely clung to the hand-painted lid.

Tsalina worked her hands down the sides of the box until she could wiggle her fingers under the bottom. It was heavier than she expected, but she was able to lean back and use her own weight to hoist it over the edge. There was no lock and the rusted hasp yielded easily. Apparently, there were several separate layers inside the box.

Someone had carefully wrapped each object in oilskin to protect it as best they could.

The first layer was heavy and she removed it with great care. It was a large Bible. Tsalina set it aside and eagerly unwrapped the next parcel. There were several stacks of letters and a leather-bound journal. Her curiosity was skipping hand-in-hand with her anticipation as she carefully opened the journal. A beautiful hand-written script greeted her eyes as she parted the fragile pages.

17 June, 1845

*Today, Taryn Learry became Taryn Sullivan as Shaine and
I were married outside of Brendan's Chapel in Tralee with
parents and friends sharing our joy. This lovely journal is a gift
from my mother, knowing that I would diligently write in its
pages the story of my life (and Shaine's) in the years to come.*

*It is with great love that I look back on the gift of schooling that
my parents gave to me when we moved from Cork to Kerry and
I was able to attend the Roman Catholic school in Clounalour.*

Shaine is waiting. I must go for now.

18 August, 1848

*Shaine and I have both worked so hard, yet we have little to
show for it. Our tiny stone cottage has been built by our own
hands, yet it is not really our own. Baron Rossmore, across the
sea in Sussex, owns the ground upon which it stands and, should
we leave, all our efforts here will remain with the land.*

*And leaving is something that weighs heavily upon us at this
time. There is a great famine throughout the land, and news
reaches us that thousands have perished for want of enough food*

to sustain them. My parents have returned to Cork, in search of better days. I miss them, but wish them well.

The rot and scale that devastates the potato has reached us here in Ardfert and what is left of our tiny crop may not see us through the winter. My turnips are fine, however, and will be so valuable as the chill sets in. We have cut and dried enough peat to meet our needs for cooking and warmth for several months ahead.

The demise of the potato may be ordained by God (as some say), but our starvation and deaths are the direct result of English greed. We raise more than enough crops to feed our people, yet they are shipped under British military guard to London and Liverpool. I have seen wagon after wagon pass through Scrahan Cross, loaded with corn, peas, beans, onions, honey and butter, as well as livestock, all to be loaded on waiting merchant ships in Barrow Harbor. Even if this bounty were to be made available to us, we could not afford to buy. There are sad days behind us, but misery ahead.

12 August, 1849

Our potatoes have failed almost entirely. We may find a handful that can be eaten, but should we try to make it through the winter, we shall surely starve.

Word has reached us from Cork that my dear mother has perished from fever brought on in her weakened condition. Neither she nor my father had eaten for three days.

We have helped to bury four neighbors since the first of the year. Now we have decided that if we are to survive, we must leave our home and village, though it rends our hearts. Shaine has been enquiring about passage to the New World, but most of the ships are sailing from Galway or Dublin.

Tears flowed from Tsalina's eyes, as she absorbed the misery in Taryn's words. She leafed ahead in the journal, could not stop reading.

20 August, 1849

Now comes good news, or at least good within the dismal circumstances which surround us. Shaine has word that the Caractacus, sailing out of Galway, will make port in Barrow Harbor on the 1st or 2nd of September, with space for a dozen additional passengers. Baron Rossmore has told us in the past that he will pay for our passage (doing whatever it takes to get us off the land) and that any ship's captain will transport us on the Baron's word. We pray that this will prove true.

4 September, 1849

Oh, how my heart aches for the home we have left behind. The blaze upon the hearth, the sturdy table that Shaine hewed from the fallen elm, my herbs and flowers waiting for springtime's call. And the view, standing at our door, across the peat bogs and bay to Derrymore and the mountains beyond. All that we have known is fading from sight as our ship, Caractacus, slides by the Blasket Islands. Will we ever see our homeland again, or will it just become a memory?

Now we are below, in steerage once more, where we scratch out a rough place to sleep — when we can. Here we cannot tell day from night and the stench is an insult to our nostrils. But our captain, bless him, has permitted twenty of us at a time to come up to the aft deck and breathe the sea air for half of an hour. Because of concern for our few meager possessions, Shaine and I will take turns climbing the ladder to the deck to breathe that refreshing air.

15 September, 1849

*We are eleven days into our voyage and have come to
know many of the others who share this foul space with us.
Unfortunately, two of the men who had boarded the ship at
Galway a week ahead of us have become gravely ill. We have
been told that the ship's medical officer — if indeed he exists —
has not the time to tend to those of us in steerage. Thus, with two
midwives, a few herbs, and a scattering of herbal knowledge, we
are left to our own devices.*

*The water is almost undrinkable. The kegs which contain it must
have been used previously for turpentine or some other noxious
fluid. We have been told that our crossing to New York will take
six weeks if the weather holds and the storms do not come upon
us. I do not see how the biscuits and sad potatoes they give us
will hold out that long. Shaine and I have already eaten the few
turnips that we dug and brought with us. Oh how I long for the
taste of a lettuce leaf from my garden!*

27 September, 1849

*Keagan and Seamus, the men from Galway who had fallen ill,
both died during the night. Typhus was the likely cause. The
crew was unwilling to touch them, so Shaine and another man
carefully wrapped them in old sail cloth, heaved them up the
ladder, and gave them a watery burial. I read two verses over
them from our family Bible, the most precious possession I have
brought with us. Since I am one of only a few here with writing
skill, I told Keagan and Seamus as they lay ill in their bunks
that I would post letters to their families should they not reach
New York alive.*

2 October, 1849

*It is hard to keep track of the passing days here below deck,
however I never miss the daily call for fresh air and this lends a
slight feeling of normality to the uncertainty of time. The view of
the ocean is rarely the same, yet it is always the same — beautiful,
but menacing.*

*We are continually hungry, but there is no recourse. Our situa-
tion is little different from the last four years at home. Three of
our company are so affected by fever that they cannot rise. The
bad air is intense. It must be full of sickness itself.*

5 October, 1849

*I thought that conditions here in steerage could get no worse, but
I was wrong. For three days we have not been allowed on deck,
as a terrible storm has taken the ship in its grip, and with the
pitch and roll of the hull, it has been impossible to sleep for more
than a few minutes at a time. Even with empty stomachs, the
retching is compelling. There is no relief.*

*Adding to the misery, we are allowed no fires and the lanterns
have been extinguished. When our lives are in the balance
though, we cannot complain, for we have all heard of the Ocean
Monarch, the ship on which my cousins Bridget and Ashling
and other Irish emigrants left from Galway last year, the ship
which caught fire and sank in the Atlantic, with 176 souls lost.*

*The crew has opened the hatch just a crack for ventilation, but it
has given me a sliver of light by which to write these words.*

6 October, 1849

*Once more, at last, we are allowed our half hour on the aft deck
and I am among the first up the ladder. It is a glorious feeling to
be alive on a calm sea with a light breeze from the east filling the*

sails. Our small group learns from the seaman at the hatch what the ship and crew have gone through for the last three days while we huddled in the blackness below.

When the wind and sea had first given warning, the captain had tried to outrun the storm, changing course to drive northwest under full sail. Hours later, when it became apparent that this was a hopeless, hazardous course of action, all hands were ordered aloft to pull in canvas and ride with the storm, leaving only enough sail for steerage.

We survived, but not without tragedy. Angus MacLeod, a young seaman from Glasgow, was thrown into the raging ocean from the height of the mainmast as he tried to untangle a line from the starboard end of the yard. Despite the efforts of his fellow crewmen, he was lost.

The captain said that the storm drove us north, putting us almost due east of Halifax, and will add at least two days to the length of our voyage.

17 October, 1849

Time for us creeps on, slow, heavy and suffocating. Five of our company have died thus far and many are sick. Shaine and I have our youth, but even that has not held at bay the chills and weakness that regularly run their course through our bodies. Lack of proper nourishment has made everyone weaker and more susceptible to sickness.

This morning I was again among the first group to take the air on the aft deck. Clouds hung low to the east and the sun rose behind us, an orange ball of fire. The first officer surprised me with a tap on the shoulder and an offer of extra food if I were to come to his cabin. Despite my body's desperate need for nourishment, I was outraged. Does he not know that Shaine and I are married? Of course he does! They will toss my starved body overboard before I will submit to his suggestions! Shane is infuriated too, but what can we do?

23 October, 1849

Shaine was on the aft deck for his break this morning when he heard the shout of "land ho!" from the crow's nest. His entire deck group rushed to the hatch to tell us the joyous news! You can imagine the pandemonium in steerage as we absorbed the long-awaited tidings! The captain says we will be at the dock in New York City by mid-afternoon, depending on the availability of a vacant berth.

I must rush to gather together what little we have.

Taryn's words had taken Tsalina into another world, a world she had never heard of, yet they had reached out to touch her heart and make her wonder even more about who Luke was. Wiping tears from her face, she imagined herself aboard the *Caractacus*, with all the uncertainties that Taryn and Shaine had experienced. They must have been related to Luke, but how, and why was Taryn's journal in Luke's cabin?

Despite the turmoil of moving into Lucas' cabin, whenever curiosity lured them away from responsibility, Tsalina's family, especially Sunrise and Lina, perused the journal and letters that she had discovered. Gradually, they pulled the pieces together into a sad, but intriguing, story.

It was Sunrise who gave a narrative voice to Lucas' life one night, after the family had finished a tasty dinner of trout and poke salad.

"I've read Taryn's journal twice, checked the generations entered in the family bible and puzzled over the letters and notes, finally tying the pieces together as best I can. I've tried to discern the timeline, and occasionally I'd find a stray note written by Taryn that shed light on her feelings. It's not a happy story.

Lina, you were captivated by the journey on the sailing ship, but wondered how the couple was related to Lucas and where they came from. Here is what I know.

"Taryn was Lucas' mother and Shaine his father.

"Their home had been near the southwest coast of Ireland, in the village of Ardfert, close to the city of Tralee. According to the family records in their Bible, which chronicled the Learry Family, Taryn's ancestors had lived in the south of Ireland for at least eight generations.

"Taryn was eighteen and Shaine was twenty when the Great Hunger forced them to flee Ireland.

"When the ship landed in New York, and they were at last free of the dark, stinking hold where they spent seven long weeks, they had few clues of where to go to find food, lodging or work.

"Apparently, they happened on a room in the Bowery that was shared with four other Irish immigrants, and Shaine hired on to load and unload ships at the nearby docks.

"But it seems that a number of factors drove them out of New York within the first year. The filth that piled up in the streets, the lack of privacy, and more than any other, the prejudice against the Irish by those who considered themselves to be 'established citizens.'

"When they left New York in 1850, they settled for a time near Harpers Ferry, where Shaine found employment with the Baltimore & Ohio Railroad in the company's push westward to connect with the trade on the Ohio River.

"I could not find the reason that Shaine and Taryn left Harpers Ferry, but I guess that with each move they came closer to feeling that they were living in the farm country they had left behind in Ireland. Or, perhaps, wanting a place of their own, land was more of a bargain down here.

"In 1857, they moved to the very piece of land where we live now. Shaine and Taryn apparently had saved enough that they could buy the land outright and build this small log house. Lucas was born in this cabin in 1858 and — surprise — Taryn gave birth to his sister Bridget two years later!

"The next year, Shaine was again offered work at higher wages by the B&O Railroad because of his previous skill and experience. Promising his family that he would return soon, he became a fore-man in the Martinsburg rail shops, just as the Civil War was starting. This brief letter from Shaine to Taryn gives us a glimpse of that time."

Martinsburg, Virginia, 4 June, 1861

My dear Taryn,

How I miss you and our little ones. Things here are not as I expected. There is much unrest and often a request to "choose sides," North or South, something I have no desire to do.

General Jackson and the Virginia Militia, two days ago took four of our locomotives and reportedly drove them to Winchester over a branch line. They then destroyed the main line bridge two miles east of here. Rumor has it that they may try to take several of the larger camelback locomotives from our shops here at Martinsburg.

I am putting in this envelope most of my first pay and will bring the second when I come home, which will be soon.

Kiss little Lucas and Bridget for me.

I love you all,
Shaine

"The next piece of the time line that I was able to place was this, a brittle yellow telegram sent from the B&O offices in Martinsburg to Taryn. Of course it must have come to Asheville first and probably then by horseback to the Sullivan farm."

Sunrise had to pause and regain her composure at this point. Blinking back tears, she read as her hand trembled.

> MARTINSBURG, VIRGINIA
> 24 JUNE, 1861
>
> TO: MRS. SHAINE SULLIVAN
> B&O RR MANAGEMENT   STOP   REGRETS DEATH   STOP
> SHAINE SULLIVAN   STOP   PERFORMING RAILROAD
> DUTIES STOP 22 JUNE, 1861
>   J. GARRETT
>   SUPERVISOR, B&O REPAIR SHOPS

"Can you imagine the icy chill of grief that gripped that young mother and two small children as her tears rained down on that unfeeling piece of paper."

Sunrise glanced up at her own family. There was only silence, and not a dry cheek anywhere.

At last, Tsalina spoke. "But what happened next? How did Taryn survive with the farm and little ones to care for?"

"We will probably never know the details, as there are not enough fragments for us to piece together. Taryn could likely not bear to write in her grief, as there are no longer any entries in her journal.

But I was just coming to the biggest heartbreak of all — the cold facts from the records in Taryn Learry's family Bible. Lucas' sister Bridget died at the age of six, probably from one of the childhood diseases that were so common in the last century. Does that loss of his young sister in her early years tell you something of Lucas' love for you, Lina?

"And then — be it by grief, despair, sickness or accident — we'll likely never know — Lucas' mother was dead at thirty-nine, barely time for Lucas to reach manhood. Lucas himself must have made the entry in the family record. Little should we wonder about the cause of his solitary and bitter life. If only we could have known of his loneliness and somehow reached out to him while he was alive."

∞

The years passed as they will, the little farm thrived, and the children grew to adulthood. Night Sky married first, he and his wife staying on to work the land. Raven felt the call of the West, studied hydrology at the University of Montana in Missoula, and later became a park ranger in the North Cascades.

And Tsalina? Of course she grew into a beautiful young woman — how could she not? Her own brand of self-schooling served her well — she often took books to peruse at the medicine wheel. But much of the time her body remained motionless, only her eyes observing the many wild creatures whose curiosity brought them close to her, their minds often connecting with her own. By the time she was fourteen, her knowledge of herbs and other wild plants, as well as animals, augmented by her detailed sketches, filled a journal that would have made Sequoyah jealous. She was, of course, fluent in the Cherokee language.

Based on an impressive learning portfolio created by Tsalina herself, she was granted admission to Western Carolina College at age fifteen.

Four years later, she rented a small cabin in Cherokee, a half hour from the farm, the deed now shared with her parents and brothers.

A dozen young men would have given their fortune to be husband or partner to Tsalina, but she would have none of it. Within her heart burned the Cherokee heritage that was sliding away from her people. She spent untold hours in the company of the remaining elders, listening to their wisdom and the tales which spanned so many generations. In turn, she created classes in Native language and history. By the time she was thirty, she had published eight books and many papers on the traditions and oral history of her people.

At thirty-five, she finally chose one of her most persistent suitors to share her life, a handsome young man with admirable values, who played one of the leading roles in the recently created Cherokee historical drama, *Unto These Hills*. But a partner and two children of her own did little to slow down her dedication to the heritage of her people. Late in her life, her people bestowed upon Tsalina the greatest possible honor, that of Beloved Woman of the Cherokee.

But through all those years, Tsalina never failed to return in October to the small knoll on the farm, where she would climb to Lucas Sullivan's final resting place and sit among the flowers of autumn, purples and yellows, beside the stone cairn she had built so long before. As she closed her eyes to turn her gaze inward, she was certain that she could feel Lucas, as well as Bridget, Taryn and Shaine smiling with her.

∞ ∞ ∞

This story arose from my desire to connect the Cherokee with those of us who have displaced them, in some small meaningful act of reconciliation. Every day, we still judge, in only our personal context, people we pass, without ever seeking out their stories.

So many families in these southern Appalachians have ancestry embracing Scotland and Ireland that it was logical to delve into the hardships which brought them to this region. The situation that Taryn describes in her part of Ireland in the 1840s, the ship *Caractacus* on which they sailed, the Civil War railroad incidents, even the sinking of Tall Bear's ship, the *Twiggs*, are all historically accurate.

And of course, some will say, "Hey, Martinsburg's in West Virginia, not Virginia!" The reply would simply be, West Virginia did not exist until 1863; prior to that year, it was all Virginia.

And is there a medicine wheel on our mountain? I have never found one there, yet I do know of one on a mountain high over Sawmill Creek, a tributary of the Little Tennessee not far from our home.

Beyond the Mountain
1994

AUTUMN WAS WISE beyond her eleven years. She wore her blond hair in a single thick braid and from her brown eyes shone an understanding of life not common in children. Yet, a child she still was.

Her family had helped. Mom and Dad, with their own hands and those of an occasional friend, had shaped their home from stone and wood to blend into their mountain cove. No bulldozer had opened wounds in the land; instead, the house flowed with the slope of the terrain, unusual, but quite pleasing to the eye. And life on the mountain was a family affair, from the work of planting, harvesting, putting by or building, to that of reading or swimming. Autumn and her brothers learned life by living it.

And there was Lost Star Rising, Autumn's closest friend. No one at school knew her by that name — she was simply Cindy Meadows to them. Her family was Cherokee — living in a modern world, but keeping alive within their own circle that knowledge from the past which gave meaning to the Native American spirit. She and Autumn shared a love for the wild places and all that lived or grew there.

This early April morning held all the promise of springtime and Autumn did not want to miss a minute of it. The air was balmy, the branch ran full from recent rains and new life was pushing up everywhere. Too much in fact, for the spring garden needed attention and that would be her task. The planting and harvesting were great fun, but the care in between was something else. "I'd better get to it though," she thought.

By lunchtime, you could see it was a garden and not a wilderness. "Mom, I've finished the weeding — even the lettuce — can I go to the top?"

"You may, Autumn, but watch your step and be back by five — I'll need you inside then."

Quickly she gathered her sketch pad, pencils and charcoal, stuffing them into her daypack. She added a sweater and apple just in case. Her trail wound steeply upward, crossing and re-crossing the creek, past a mighty beech and three white oaks that had somehow escaped the logger's ax a half-century earlier.

Forty minutes later she stood, breathing heavily, on a rock outcropping that overlooked the sprawling valley below. The Little Tennessee River shone silver in the distance and the wispy cirrus clouds did little to disturb the warm sunshine on her face. It was one of her favorite spots for solitude.

But today it seemed that houses — too many of them — stared back from every hillside. "If people must build in the most beautiful spots, why can't they at least live here year round?" she wondered. "And there's the Cowee Valley Mall — I hadn't realized you could see any of it from here." She had shed bitter tears when Rickman's general store had been leveled to make way for the mall.

"No, this will never do," she murmured to herself as she shouldered her daypack again. "I should have gone right to the Bear Cave Falls to begin with." It was one of the secrets that she and Lost Star Rising shared. She could be at the cave within the hour.

Autumn was almost there when the front passed through. Her sweater felt good as the clouds thickened and the temperature began to plummet. She was tired and knew she should turn back now, but it was only two-fifteen and she was so close.

There it was — a small opening partially screened by laurel, just past a natural saddle in the ridge. Here the valley was not so wide and the distant houses sparse. Autumn slipped past the rocks, and bent slightly as she entered.

Waiting for her eyes to adjust, she could just see light at the far end of the cave. A thin curtain of water nearly covered the second opening as the falls plunged another thirty feet to the rocks below. Lost Star

Rising and her family considered this a sacred place, as had untold generations before them.

Seating herself on the bare earth where she could see the falling water and the dim outlines beyond, Autumn dug into her pack. She had never come here alone before, but had wanted to sketch this place ever since her first visit with Lost Star Rising.

She drew for a long while, yet felt she had not captured the true spirit of this ancient gathering spot. Gradually she realized that she was quite cold, even with the sweater — and hungry, too, having eaten the apple before she had reached the falls. Quickly, she packed her sketches and made her way back to the entrance.

A mama black bear could not have startled her the way the falling snow did. There were already four inches on the ground and the world she thought she knew so well seemed lost in the swirling gusts of white. A blizzard?! In April?! She plunged into the storm and in two minutes could identify nothing familiar.

"This is stupid, Autumn," she growled to herself. "Get back to the cave before your footprints are gone." She stumbled again through the

opening with a sinking feeling in her heart. No matches. No food. She tried covering herself with leaves to stop the chills, but the leaves were as damp as her sweater. She closed her eyes tight and concentrated on home — the faces, the voices … warmth.

Her mind was suddenly and sharply aware of being in the cave. She must have slept. But how long? Rising, she thrust her head outside and saw the valley in twilight — a springtime green and not a flake of snow in sight. But her body still ached from chills and hunger.

"Now this is strange," Autumn thought. "The mountains, hills and streams look the same, but … there is not a house to be seen anywhere. Only a small fire burning near the bend of that creek below. And I *know* this path to the valley wasn't here when I came."

It took but a short time to descend to where she could hear the happy voices of Cherokee children playing and savor the smell of venison and corn roasting. Yet the creek, swift and wide, lay between her and the others. As if she were invisible, they took no notice of her.

The hand on her shoulder was gentle and the voice was calm.

"What brings you to us, granddaughter? Your time in this valley has not yet come."

"Oh grandfather, I came from the cave and need food, and the warmth of your fire!"

"You cannot cross that barrier." The voice that reached into her world was firm.

"And I want to go home!"

"There is a way."

The shaman stepped to the edge of the water and motioned to Autumn. "Your path starts here."

The creek bed seemed alive with beautiful pebbles and flashes of gold. Autumn thrust her arm into the icy water and closed her fingers around a smooth flat stone. It was of a reddish hue not common in rocks of the East and fit the palm of her hand as if it had grown there. "You have chosen well," said the shaman.

What happened next seemed both real and unreal, but ever after shrouded in mist — the grinning face of Forest, her teenage brother, bending over her — dry clothing and a down quilt — the strong arms of Dad, a bear of a man — the crunch of boots in deep snow — a full moon floating somewhere above.

Reality flooding back beside the woodstove of home. Steaming cider and hot blueberry cobbler. Mom's tear-stained face. A thousand questions. The clock striking three in the morning. The dream, haunting and beautiful. And a red stone, with the feel of satin, that clattered to the floor as her fingers relaxed.

∞   ∞   ∞

The setting for this bit of fiction is the mountain area surrounding the Little Tennessee River valley in western North Carolina. We call it home.

Tom Rickman's general store still stands, as did Tom himself (at 95) when I wrote this story. There is no Cowee Valley Mall, thank God! But on our mountain there really is a Bear Cave Falls with a ten-foot curtain of falling water. Some of our heaviest snowfalls (24 to 30 inches) have come in April. And, of course, Autumn does have a smooth red stone that fits her palm perfectly.

And there is even a backstory to the backstory, which I was not aware of until I read George Ellison's newly published book on Horace Kephart's life, *Back of Beyond* last year.

On page 190 of his book, as Ellison describes how Babe Burnett hid out after the shooting of Hol Rose, I was startled to realize that it is quite likely that he wintered on our mountain! We live in the watershed where Caler Cove Branch rises, there being several springs that come together to form the creek and a half mile of our highest property line runs with the Macon/Swain county line.

We often hike from our place over the mountain and down into Brush Creek. On one of the spring feeds, there is a place we call the Bear Cave Falls, where a thin curtain of water falls, but most of the shallow cave is dry, providing a primitive shelter of sorts. Access is difficult, requiring a steep ascent of the last quarter mile. Few people would find it without knowing ahead of time where it was located. And I would not have wanted to spend the winter there!

Frank and Etta Browning, who provided food and other necessities to Burnett as he hid, were our neighbors, but had passed on before we came to the mountain in 1982. Their property bordered ours, and it's good to know that Frank and Etta helped Babe and eventually convinced him to give himself up.

Bear With Us
1995

IT WAS AN EYE OPENER. Nobody could argue with that. Like Pearl said, "Nothing like this has ever happened in our valley! Even Pink's snakebite couldn't hold a candle to the ruckus Essie's run caused."

For those of you who might not remember, Pink was sitting in his rocker on the front porch of his cabin when he was bitten in the hand by a flying snake head. It seems his grandson was mowing the yard when he spotted the copperhead and with great glee shredded it on his next pass. Pink's hand was stiff as a board for a month, but other than being a little more ornery than usual, he seemed to have undergone no ill effects. The snake could not make the same claim.

Essie had caused a bit of a stir when she moved to the settlement. She had bought Zeb's cabin up in the cove, which included ten acres of mountain hardwoods that backed up to government land.

"T'aint no place for a lone lady," Texas had said. "Livin' that far back, she needs a man to take care o' matters."

But that was five years ago. Esther Mae Patton had proved them all wrong. She appeared able to handle any challenge that mountain living might bring. At least, until that fateful Sunday morning.

Zeb's cabin was rather stark and not long on amenities, but it was well placed to catch the winter sun. The early settlers knew what they were doing when it came to passive solar, even if they didn't call it by that name. Essie had made some changes, not the least of which was bringing the plumbing indoors. A spring, higher up the mountain, provided gravity water and Essie had rigged up an old water heater tank, coils of black pipe and a glass covered box to provide plenty of hot water, courtesy of the sun.

The cabin had small windows and tended to be dark inside, so when she replaced the cedar shakes on the roof, Essie installed two large skylights to brighten up the place. "She's a right handy lady, she is," Texas had had to admit when he hauled the cast iron bathtub up the mountain in his pickup and helped her wrestle it into place beneath one of the skylights. Essie had just finished splitting nearly two cords of firewood that morning.

But even though the community grudgingly had to admit that Essie seemed to know what she was doing, she remained, in their view, a pretty strange character. As a writer, she spent many hours alone at her cabin and, to her neighbors, seemed to have no visible source of income. This alone was enough to generate strange rumors.

That was not all. She had gently but firmly declined several invitations to the Needmore Baptist Church even though the church was only half a mile down the road, the closest place to hers. Essie had given no hint of her own faith or affiliation and Annie Nell had confided to several of her friends in the local homemakers group, "I just *know* she's one of those *New Agers*! And what's more, she doesn't eat meat!"

But they had to admit, at age 43, she was in much better shape than any of her critics. More than once, Annie Nell's husband had nearly put the tractor in the ditch while watching Essie pass by on her morning run down the valley. She usually ran early, and this was particularly important on Sundays, since she had to go right past the church and didn't wish to offend any of her neighbors.

It was September and high canning season for most of the settlement. Essie had put by almost four dozen quarts of string beans and had also made applesauce from the apples in Zeb's old orchard. On the cabin roof, she had rigged up a solar drier for thin apple slices, covered with a layer of cheesecloth to discourage thieving birds.

∞

For Brimstone, a 300-pound black bear in her fifth autumn, it had not been a good year. Her son Quicknose, now two, had left to follow his own pursuits and she had been without cubs for two seasons.

A development called Harmony Grove had been built smack in the middle of what was once her favorite blueberry patch, and this fall's acorn crop was the sparsest in thirty years.

Thus it was that Brimstone's hunger drew her down the mountain to Essie's cove. At first it was the small orchard that attracted her attention, but she soon found there were no apples left within easy reach. Even so, her keen nose told her that for sure there were more nearby and she lumbered toward the cabin to investigate. It took but a few moments to shinny up the white oak and gingerly transfer her weight to the cabin roof, where the sliced apples were drying.

The pitch of the roof where Brimstone made this first transition was fairly gentle. However, the roof slope where the apples were drying became considerably steeper and it was here that she lost it. As her claws ripped out of the shakes, Brimstone made a last futile lunge for the apples, but instead took a tumbling plunge down the roof.

∞

Essie was pleased with herself. It was a fine Sunday morning, the air was cool and her run had been exceptionally fast. She kicked off her running shoes, popped a Loreena McKennitt CD into the stereo, and drew a full tub of water. The temperature was a bit too hot, so she went to the kitchen for a bowl of granola while she anticipated the relaxing soak.

Slipping out of her running outfit, Essie tossed it into the hamper and grabbed a fresh towel. She pushed aside the door curtain to the bathroom and took one step inside. It was at this moment that Brimstone also entered the bathroom.

When a 300-pound bear bursts through your skylight in a shower of glass and ends up in the bath you were about to enjoy, it takes a moment to grasp the situation. But not many moments! As Brimstone stood up in the tub with a bellow and looked Essie in the eye, the decision was immediate. Essie dropped the towel and was outta there!

And from Brimstone's point of view? Well, when you've just taken an unexpected fall, cut your foot and find yourself in hot water, you might be inclined to blame present company! She made a lunge for Essie, slipped on the edge of the tub and ended up with one hind leg caught in the commode. With a roar of frustration, she tried to disengage, and ended up ripping the toilet out of its moorings.

This gave Essie just the lead she needed. She was through the cabin door and down the road like a shot, Brimstone a hundred feet behind. They were pretty evenly matched, what with Brimstone having a one-toilet handicap!

Some say that Essie set a new Olympic record for the 800-meter run that day, and if Hiram had been on his tractor, he would have dropped his eyeballs. But when Deacon Birch looked up and saw Essie approaching, it was not her running that was on his mind! He was about to shout to the parson that *now* something had to be done about this outrageous lady, but he didn't have time. He suddenly realized Essie wasn't running *past* the church, she was running *into* it!

"Don't look!" screamed Mattie Sue as she clapped a hand over her husband Sam's eyes. The fact that they were still underway in the church parking lot didn't really register until their Chevy came to rest ten yards inside the graveyard.

The early teen Sunday Schoolers were just finishing up in the vestibule. "Even your innermost thoughts cannot be hidden. We all stand naked before the Lord," the teacher admonished. As Essie burst through the front doors, the class self-destructed.

About this time, Brimstone rounded the corner, still sporting the toilet. Texas had just eased his pickup into the lot, took one look, and reached for his gun rack. "You can't!" gasped his wife, "It's Sunday, we're at church, and it's not even bear season yet!"

"The hell I can't," growled Texas. "This is self-defense!" He squeezed off a round from the .30-06.

Fortunately for Brimstone, the shot hit squarely on the commode, shattering it in a hundred pieces. Suddenly free, and rapidly retreating from the rifle shot, she accelerated to top speed, bursting through the barbed wire of the Breedlove pasture, scattering cows in all directions. This act probably saved her life, as Texas couldn't get off another shot without endangering his neighbor's livelihood. As for Brimstone, she had already decided it was her last visit to the Needmore Community.

Deacon Birch and Parson Savage were frozen like pillars of salt. It was Sidney Jane, the choir director who saved the moment, snatching a spare robe from the choir closet and tossing it to Essie, whose awareness was just now catching up with her trembling body.

Some late arrivals that morning said they had never heard the choir sing so sweetly and the new voice added a lot.

Parson Savage always regretted not having seized the moment for an on-the-spot baptism.

The Bryson boys, who had never before seen a naked woman anywhere, regarded it as answered prayer.

As for Essie, she built an indoor dehydrator that week.

∞ ∞ ∞

While I was away biking and photographing grizzlies in Alaska, a large black bear visited our home in North Carolina for four days in a row, watching the kids through the picture windows on ground level and nosing around the residue of apple butter making, which had been dumped near the front deck.

When I later got on the roof to clean the chimneys, I found that the bear had been there too. She had stepped off the mountain onto our bathroom roof, which has a gentle pitch, and torn out several shakes near the large skylight which is directly above our bathtub.

For some reason she had climbed from there to the steeper part of the roof and made it almost to the ridge. But at that point she slipped and left deep claw marks for about ten feet down the shakes, to a point where she must have either somersaulted or rolled the rest of the way.

Envisioning "what might have happened" gave birth to this bit of fiction!

And yes, the Needmore Baptist Church is fictional. I didn't want to send a naked lady into the Hightower or Maple Springs congregations unannounced!

A Road Not Traveled
1997

"LAURA! DON'T FORGET I NEED TWO MORE EGGS RIGHT AWAY!" It was Mom calling, and for the moment, I had forgotten. Adding a handful of oats to Dolly's feed bucket, I scooped up the basket of eggs I had collected earlier and headed for the house.

"Coming!" I replied, and in a moment I was in the warm kitchen where Mom was mixing the batter for Connie's birthday cake. My little sister, always an early riser, was drawing scary faces in the windowpane frost while she waited to lick the beaters. She was turning three tomorrow, and the cake would be hers.

I could hear the ax rhythmically hitting the chopping block as Brent, the older of my two younger brothers, split kindling on the side porch. The smell of those freshly cut pieces of red oak was as familiar to me as the steamy odors of the barn. It spoke of winter coming, hot apple cider at the kitchen table, the root cellar full of the year's toil, extra quilts on my bed and time for family games while the snow shut out the rest of the world.

Clint, my nine-year-old brother, was still in the clawfoot bathtub, stretching his time as far as he could. Dad had already left for Gene Owenby's sawmill in the old pickup truck. He would return soon with a load of rough-cut lumber for a new stall in the barn.

I knew that Dolly, our Guernsey cow, would be impatient as I stepped back into the crisp morning air to return to the barn. Our five cats fell into step beside me as soon as they heard the clank of the milk bucket swinging on its hasp.

Dolly twisted her head in the stanchion, giving me that "it's about time" look and indeed, from the size of her udder, she was certainly ready for some relief. I sponged her off and hunkered down on the milking stool, hoping that this wouldn't be a morning that she would put a hoof in the bucket.

Lining up in the stall opposite my position, the cats knew what was in store. Having milked Dolly by hand for five years, I had acquired certain bovine related skills. I could hit an unsuspecting observer in the eye at ten feet with a warm squirt and my brothers had learned to be somewhere else at milking time.

But the cats felt differently. They eyed me expectantly from the opposite side of Dolly's belly as I positioned the bucket and nestled my cheek in her flank. They knew that every now and then I would try to squirt them in the ear, but it mattered not. They would guzzle the warm milk whenever they could get their mouths lined up with the stream and when I was finished, they would relax in the straw, cleaning each other's fur.

As I walked back toward the house, I could hear the lower gears whining in Dad's pickup as he climbed the hill on Old North Road before he turned into our lane. He must have quite a load today.

When Dad was about my age, there had been a push by the local government and developers to "upgrade" Old North Road into a big high-speed thoroughfare. Fortunately, for us and our neighbors, community opinion had prevailed and Old North remained a friendly country road.

Dad pulled up near the corner of the barn and I knew he would expect Brent and me to help him unload the lumber. I heard Brent shout, and at the same time his friend Tristan leaped from the truck. I hadn't known he was coming. The boys were both twelve and acted as if they owned the county when they were together. It was a relief when Dad said, "Laura, Brent and Tristan can handle this job. Why don't you see what Mom needs at the house?"

Just then, Mom appeared at the truck with a basket of freshly baked cookies and a jug of the cider we had pressed last week.

"Here, Carl, take the big mug. You must be thirsty after loading all that lumber," smiled Mom.

"Thanks, Alice. That really hits the spot!"

Later that afternoon, I took a good book, pen, paper and a snack in my daypack and climbed to the treehouse. The sun had driven the chill from the air and this spot, overlooking a small waterfall, was one of my favorites for inspiration. If I were lucky, I might have an hour undisturbed, since Connie and Clint were helping Mom, and Brent was trading baseball cards with Tristan in his room.

I finished the chapter that I had been reading in Mists of Avalon, closed my eyes, and leaned back against the trunk of the huge poplar that supported the treehouse. Try as I might, I could not keep my mind on the story I had been trying to put on paper this week. Dan's smile kept creeping into my mind to send any other thoughts running for cover.

I hadn't known until recently that boys were made this way. Dan had been around ever since I could remember, but all of a sudden it was as if he had turned into someone else — someone who might even know the mysteries of life. He would bring me a pebble that shone like the moon or take me to a spot where pink ladyslippers were blooming beside the branch. I would turn sixteen next week, but never in my life had I felt my insides flutter the way they did when Dan spoke!

He would be there tonight, at the Lonesome Creek Community Center, for the square dance and potluck. My legs wouldn't stay still, just thinking about the dance. In fact, I thought, I'd better head for the tub now if I'm going to have any hot water. The whole family will be going tonight and the last ones to clean up usually have a chilly time of it!

I slipped into the colorful party dress that I had sewed three weeks ago and stood in front of the mirror, brushing my hair and trying to decide whether to wear it up or down. Finally, I decided on one thick braid down my back. It would stay in place better during some of the twirls and moves.

Mom was just pulling a mouth-watering vegetable pie from the oven and Dad had his fiddle out of the case, checking that all was in order. "Grandma called and would like us to bring her a small basket of Winesaps. Everything went into cider last Tuesday, so they'll need to be picked. Laura, would you?"

"Sure, Mom," though I knew the only apples left were in the higher branches. "I wish she had asked while I was still in my jeans," I thought as I headed for the orchard. The sun was just about to drop behind the ridge and I could feel the chill in the air already.

Fortunately, the ladder still rested against the upper branches of one of the Winesap trees. Hooking the basket over one arm, I scrambled up within reach of the apples, only to find that some were beginning to rot and the birds had been at work on others. I had to stretch to find enough good ones.

"We see England, we see France…" It was Brent and Tristan, grinning at the bottom of the ladder. "We see Laura's under…" Splat!! A rotten apple caught Brent squarely in the forehead as Tristan dived for cover! I hadn't been shortstop on the high school softball team last spring for nothing. Younger brothers — blah!

My basket was nearly full anyhow. There was a beep from the van, which meant Mom and Dad were ready to go. I scrambled down the ladder and the three of us dashed out of the orchard and squeezed into the rear seats with Connie and Clint and the hot casserole.

It was a curvy ride and the boys kept trying to mash me against the side of the van whenever a bend in the road came my way. But my mind wasn't on the horseplay — it was looking ahead to the dance. In ten minutes we were there, a crescent moon hanging over the ridge to the west, and warm light streaming out of the community center windows. My heart was already dancing.

∞

But wait! Something is wrong — dreadfully wrong. I am not here. This is not my life. I mean … it would have been my life, but I never lived. Neither did Brent and Clint and Connie. The Lonesome Creek Community Center was bulldozed twenty-three years ago when they widened and straightened Old North. You see, Alice, the girl that would have been my mother, was killed waiting for the school bus on a crisp fall morning back in '95. She thought she had time to rescue her kitten from the highway, but the road had changed — drivers could hit 75 if they had a mind to, and this one did.

The high school was in shock that day, but no one more so than Carl, who, with his fiddle, used to accompany Alice as she sang Scottish ballads. As it was, he never married, but stayed on to work the family farm and would only now and then play his fiddle at the Old Cowee School for some community event. At times such as these, his music would fill the room while his mind went far away, seeking desperately for a future that never was. But now and again — in the shifting mist of that alternate future — he would glimpse his Alice … and some-times his Connie, Clint, Brent and Laura. It is only there that I exist.

∞ ∞ ∞

Highway 28 North, out of Franklin, NC, is a two-lane country road that winds its way through the valley of the Little Tennessee River. It generally follows the contour of the surrounding mountains, serving as a feeder to the town rather than a connector to anywhere else. In 1990, a proposal to widen and straighten this road was assigned a project number and incorporated into the State's Transportation Improvement Plan). Preliminary engineering had been funded.

Knowing what effect the road would have on our rural way of life and suspecting that the real push behind it was simply big money (the creation of a second direct high-speed route to the gambling in Cherokee), many of us in the community fought the project over the next decade — fought it hard and successfully.

The project no longer exists — the Little Tennessee Land Trust (Mainspring) and the Needmore Tract now stand in its way — but no victory of this kind is ever permanent without continuing vigilance. This piece of fiction arose out of my feelings for our way of life in the Cowee, Rose Creek, Oak Grove, Burningtown, Tellico and Needmore communities.

∞

The project has indeed again come to life in the form of R-4440. Though R-4440 is only a portion of the original proposal, it strikes at the heart of the corridor, advocating the paving — with all the attendant right-of-way modification — of the gravel section of the Needmore Road. Few roads of this character now exist in the East. Needmore, an unpaved, winding country road hugs the Little Tennessee River for three and a half miles, limiting through-traffic simply by its character. Motorcycles avoid the gravel, what little traffic there is travels slowly and accidents are a rarity. This stretch of road protects an area which you might call a backwater in time, with spur roads named High Lonesome, Rattlesnake, Bull Hollow, Licklog, Panther Branch, and so on.

This, of course, is my own opinion. Many of those that live in the immediate corridor, or commute over the gravel section of road, see a benefit in having it paved. Yet the North Carolina Department of Transportation does not deviate from their uniform road building standards, whether the road be in the flatlands of the North Carolina coast, or in the tight contours of our mountains. By the time all rights-of-way and the attendant destruction are taken into account, a rare treasure will have been permanently lost.

Acknowledgments

LYNN WOODWARD, known affectionately in our family as Cricket, is my firstborn, and has been my mainstay in publishing three books. She is a photographer, artist and website designer, now sharing her time between Sisters, Oregon and Franklin, North Carolina. In her time out West, she also plays and sings with her band, the Anvil Blasters. Her work in cover and book design, proofing, and transforming the whole production into a form the printer can recognize, has been invaluable.

LIBBY HEDSTROM, my little sister, grew up on the family farm in Glenwood, Maryland, surrounded by ponies, sheep and geese. She took after our mother, Margaret, in becoming a master storyteller. It was only natural that I ask her for her critique and ideas when writing these stories. It was a delight to receive her input in bringing the characters to life. More recently, Lib is a blossoming watercolor artist.

Ciara Holden
illustrator

CIARA HOLDEN is a young mountain woman who calls Macon County home and who could have stepped right out of almost any of these tales. As an early teen, she has already developed her skills as an artist, a maker of wooden toys and a farmer with chore responsibility for her family's herd of cattle. The sketches in this book represent her first formal venture with pen & ink. Look for more of her artistry in the future.

Doug Woodward
author

DOUG WOODWARD has lived nearly forty years at the southern end of the Needmore river corridor and holds a deep love for this part of the Appalachian Mountain country. His wife and children also appreciate the generations that have lived here before them — their history, hardships and stories. Their descendants are now neighbors and friends of the author and his family in this sparsely settled country.